AMONG
THE
PEOPLE

KEITH ROMMEL

HELLBENDER
BOOKS

an imprint of Sunbury Press, Inc.
Mechanicsburg, PA USA

an imprint of Sunbury Press, Inc.
Mechanicsburg, PA USA

For information about special discounts for bulk purchases, please contact Sunbury Press Orders Dept. at (855) 338-8359 or orders@sunburypress.com.

To request one of our authors for speaking engagements or book signings, please contact Sunbury Press Publicity Dept. at publicity@sunburypress.com.

ISBN: 978-1-62006-416-0 (Trade paperback)

FIRST HELLBENDER BOOKS EDITION: April 2018

Product of the United States of America
0 1 1 2 3 5 8 13 21 34 55

Set in Bookman Old Style
Designed by Crystal Devine
Cover by Lawrence Knorr
Cover image by Maai Kaare
Edited by Jennifer Cappello

Continue the Enlightenment!

Pronounced
Sar•der•v•al

Isaiah 14:12-14
"How you are fallen from heaven, O Day Star, son
of Dawn! How you are cut down to the ground, you
who laid the nations low! You said in your heart, 'I
will ascend to heaven; above the stars of God I will
set my throne on high; I will sit on the mount of as-
sembly in the far reaches of the north; I will ascend
above the heights of the clouds; I will make myself
like the Most High."

Than•a•tol•o•gy | noun

The scientific study of death and dying and the practices associated with it, including the study of the needs of the terminally ill and their families.

DERIVATIVES
thanatological | adjective
thanatologist |-jist| noun
ORIGIN mid 19th cent.: from Greek *thanatos* *'death'* + -logy.

CHAPTER 1

THE STAIRWELL

Present Day

"You bastard!" Sardurvial said, and spat blood. He wiped his chin and tried to repress the memories that pained him deeper than any wound the beating might have left on his body. But it was fresh and flooded his mind.

"Aramus," he growled, and the sound of his name rolled off of his tongue like the sting from a slap. "You've betrayed me."

Certain that Aramus's anger is what frenzied the mob that attacked him, he couldn't understand his motivation.

"Why did you do this to me?"

Collapsing to his knees and flopping to his side, he was unable to move another inch. Thankful he escaped those who nearly beat him to death, he continued to reflect on the moment.

It all happened so fast he barely had time to react. His attempt to flee was a desperate one, but they caught him. And when they did, they kicked and punched him and shouted their hate for him. The assault was merciless and the faces that looked back at him were distorted by rage.

"Why?" he said.

Flashes of the moment played inside his mind, and with it sparks of pain coursed through his body. But in his pain there was one little victory.

"I got away from you," he said, and his limbs shook. "You became arrogant and careless and because of that I'll live to fight another day."

Knowing full well his victory might be ephemeral, he deemed it the perfect time to do something way overdue. Forcing himself to his knees and lifting trembling hands to his chin, every movement was with great struggle. He interlaced his blood-caked fingers, closed his eyes, and rested his brows on his white-knuckled hands.

"Lord, please, I beg you for forgiveness," he said, his voice echoing in the small cement space like someone reciting the prayer with him. "I've betrayed you and deserve nothing but your wrath. But if there is a way for me to redeem myself, to serve your will, I beg for that chance. I won't disappoint you again."

Feeling the invisible weight of guilt being lifted off of his shoulders, Sardurvial sighed in relief. He fell to his back again and with a snicker, he submitted himself to destiny.

"How bad could death be for someone with a soul as black as my own?" he said.

To be done with this life and all of its miseries would be a relief. One he might not deserve, but it would be better than an eternity of suffering.

Unsure if he could ever gain forgiveness for the things he had done, he trembled at the memories. Torture, torment and death were but a few of the horrible things he influenced on others.

The remembrance of the lake of fire and the everlasting pain it brought made him whimper.

"Maybe that is where I am headed, cast there to pay for the things I have done," he said, and a shiver rocked his body. "Please Lord, let me live so I can serve you. I now know I have work that I must do in your name."

If the prayer did nothing more than free his mind for the moment, it still felt right. The release brought him to silent tears because he knew if he wasn't forgiven, then that was exactly what he deserved.

He was exhausted and needed to rest and couldn't resist its call much longer. His eyelids felt as heavy as stones and his head buzzed with the pull of sleep. Maybe if he were to give in to sleep it would help heal his body, but he knew there was a chance that he might not wake from his slumber because of his injuries. Or maybe one of the members of the frenzied mob tracked him to the ice-cold shadows of the derelict stairwell he hid in and waited for him to sleep.

Maybe . . .

The thought of being vulnerable frightened Sardurvial. The chance he took by closing his eyes was something he hadn't had to worry about in a long time and he tried to fight the exhaustion.

But he soon submitted, too tired to care about his fear or the consequences of getting some rest. There would be plenty of time to worry about that after he woke.

The constant question of both present and future consumed him and exhausted his mind. He sunk into a deep sleep and began to feel the peace he had been seeking. And there, within the sanctity of his mind, he remained oblivious to the world and the dangers that awaited him: dangers that were both tangible and concealed.

CHAPTER 2

STRANGE ENCOUNTERS

Friday, October 14th, 1:00 am

Kathy held in a sneeze that shook her body and awakened the pain in her lower back. Flashes of agony arced through her body and buckled her knees. A layer of sweat instantly covered her skin and she gasped as she tried to draw breath, but the unrelenting pain within fought to control her and keep her down.

"I won't let you win," she said. "I'm okay."

She moved against it, determined to not let the past dictate her future.

As if someone had turned off a switch inside, the pain faded to a dull ache as she stood upright.

"This will not define me," she said, and continued to work with a determination to insert a sense of normalcy back into her life. Pulling the corner of a clean sheet over the edge of an unoccupied bed, she ran her hand over its cool surface to smooth it out. Retrieving two pillows she had placed on the visitor's chair, she fluffed them and placed them at the head of the bed.

"I'm okay," she reassured herself, her voice a whisper.

Walking to a bed in the back of the room where a patient slept, the complete absence of pain made her pause.

"You see, you're fine," she said. Bending to retrieve the patient's chart that hung on the footboard, the pain came again and it was strong.

"Ah," she grunted and was stuck in a bent position, holding onto the foot of the bed to keep from falling, unable to straighten herself out. Her eyes welled with tears and she fought it, but it held her firmly in place.

"Are you okay nurse?" the faceless patient said, shrouded in darkness.

"I'm fine," she struggled to say, and her own words didn't sound believable—even to herself. "I'm okay, really," she said, this time with more authority. She waited a moment before she dared to move again. Taking the chart, she studied it and hung it back up. Withdrawing a pair of latex gloves out of her pocket, she moved delicately as she positioned herself beside the patient.

"Just relax," she said gently, and took his blood pressure and administered a needle to help him with his pain. After she jotted her activities on the log and hung it back up, she walked away from the patient's bed, stiff and unsure if moving was a good idea.

"Sorry to have disturbed you," Kathy said, and disposed of the needle inside a hazardous box mounted on the wall and dropped the latex gloves into a trashcan.

Kathy exited the room and the door closed behind her. Over the PA system, a soft female voice announced that there was a telephone call for Nurse Kathy Odonnell in the recovery ward.

"Great," she said, and looked down the long hallway and sighed with apprehension, uncertain if she could make the long journey back to the nurse's station.

"This might have been a mistake," she said to herself and mindlessly admired the floors lustrous shine as she hobbled along. Her shoes squeaked on the highly polished floor, and she shook her head. "Maybe I shouldn't have come back to work so soon."

But deep down inside she knew it was what needed to be done to fight the loneliness that had abruptly entered her life. The isolation was an invisible demon that encased her in silence and self-doubt. It was big and bad and it pulled her down and lay on top of her with all of its crushing weight. It had gotten to the point where she could no longer breathe and had to get out of the house. Caring for people in need was what she loved to do and was the perfect distraction.

When she arrived at the nurses station, Claire, the head nurse, was busy sorting through a stack of papers that cluttered her desktop.

"It's your sister on line six," Claire said. "And don't worry, she's fine."

Kathy offered Claire a smile of appreciation that was filled with doubt. She hadn't heard from her sister in more than two weeks and found herself a bit nervous about the nature of her call. Her sister's past had been consumed with so much drama that Kathy only expected more every time she heard from her.

Leaning against the countertop, she picked up the phone and pressed the button labeled line six. "Hello?"

"Hello, Kathy, it's Megan." Her sister's voice boomed through the phone and sounded upbeat. "How are you doing?"

"My back hurts like hell," Kathy said, breathing heavily and unable to match the enthusiastic tone. "And I can't wait to get into bed and get off my feet."

"I'm sorry to hear that. I don't want to harp on this because I'm sure you're hearing it from everyone, but

I think you should've waited a little longer before you went back to work."

"As the week has dragged on I've thought that myself. But life goes on, you know? I've got to try and move past this."

"But your body is still healing. Don't push yourself so hard and be patient with yourself."

"I can't sit at home any longer," she said, and grimaced at the inert ache that wrenched somewhere deep inside her lower back. "Besides, I would rather deal with the physical pain than the silence of an empty house. That's beyond horrible."

"I wish there was something I could say or do to help you though this. I think you've been through enough," Megan said.

Kathy nodded and twirled the phone chord with her pointer finger. "I think we both have."

"Amen to that."

"Listen, do you mind if I called you back tomorrow? My shift is over and I want to get out of here as soon as I possibly can."

"Sure, but I just need to know if you'd be able to watch Jaiden tomorrow night? I was invited out by the girls and I need to let them know if I was able to find a babysitter and you're the only one I really trust with him at this point."

A sense of relief filled Kathy that this wasn't a call about another great tragedy.

"Of course I'll watch him."

"Thank you."

Kathy smiled. "I'm happy to hear you're finally getting out of the house, too. Who knows, maybe you'll find yourself a Prince Charming!"

Megan laughed. "No, but thank you. My last Prince Charming turned out to be a toad."

Kathy chuckled at the understatement. "Speaking of Prince Charming, have you heard from him?"

"Who, Ted?"

"Yeah, that's him, the toad."

A crackling sound inserted itself into their conversation, creating an awkward silence.

"I'm sorry Megan, I didn't mean to sound so harsh," Kathy said. "I was making a joke."

"I know, and I'm sorry. It was funny though," Megan said. "You've helped me a lot with him and you've earned the right to poke fun. To answer your question, yes, he's called and has tried to convince me he's been going to anger management and counseling. But those are just words and they don't mean a thing to me because he's completely destroyed what little trust I had left in him. You above anyone know how many times he's bruised me and I've forgiven him. I can't anymore. I've just had enough."

She began to cry.

"Listen Megan, I didn't mean to upset you," Kathy said. "You called me about something good and I spoiled it."

"No, it's okay," she said. "We haven't spoken about this in a long time and it needed to come out. I'm the one that's dragged you into the middle of it and I'm sure you worry."

"I do," Kathy said.

"Well, you don't need to anymore. I'm over him and the only thing that concerns me now is Jaiden and his feelings," Megan said. "The hardest part is when Jaiden asks me when his father is going to be able to come home. I don't know how to answer that when I know the answer is never."

"That's heart wrenching Megan. I feel bad for you and Jaiden. He's such a good kid and he's stuck in the middle of this."

"He has a heart of gold and I can see the hope in his eyes. It's so hard."

"I'm so sorry Megan," Kathy said.

"I have to remind myself that he really is just a kid and this has to be hard on him. I couldn't imagine how much he misses his father, and if I were him, I would probably blame me for everything that's happened. He doesn't understand our adult problems."

Kathy felt a sudden surge of anger conjure a harsh tone. "You know they are Ted's problems Megan, not yours. He's the one that hits you and calls you every name in the book."

"Yeah, I get that." She breathed heavily into the phone. "That's why I got an order of protection against him. What I'm trying to say is that I have to take Jaiden's feelings into consideration. It is my responsibility as his mother to protect him."

Kathy took a moment to absorb her sister's words and her anger morphed into a sense of humility. She understood why Megan had to include Jaiden's feelings in every decision she made and felt silly having even challenged it.

"I'm sorry Megan. It must be difficult being a single parent and having a child that isn't able to comprehend what you're going through. I don't mean to push the issue with Ted. It's just that I don't want to see you go through that again. The hell he put you through hurt me too and I'm not ashamed to tell you that I'm bitter about it."

"Kathy?"

"Just hear me out. Please accept my apology. With all of this pain I'm in I'm not myself tonight. I'll see you tomorrow night when you come to drop Jaiden off."

"I know you are concerned for my well being and I appreciate that," Megan said. "I love you too. I'll see you tomorrow around six."

Kathy hung up the telephone and made her way to the coat rack with a slight bend in her back and a hobble to her every step. She grabbed hold of her pink sweater and put it on. She hugged its softness and sniffed its scent. The idea of finding warmth on a chilly night reminded her of her husband Rocco. Such a tough name for such a gentle man. The security of being in his arms was the most comforting memory of them all.

And even though she only imagined she could feel the frigid air outside, she missed the romance and emotional connection she had with Rocco. Like Megan, Kathy believed she might never experience it again. Thinking about Rocco and Ted, she understood to love someone was to accept pain. But the pain, much like her sorrow, was something she couldn't bear much more of.

Kathy turned to Claire and pushed aside the lingering pain and memories. "I haven't been sleeping well and I've been counting the days away until my two nights off."

Claire continued to shuffle through papers on her desktop. She hummed her response and pushed her eyeglasses up her nose with her pointer finger. "You've put a lot of hours in and I've watched you suffer through every minute of it. I'd be lying if I didn't tell you that I was starting to think you were overdoing it for your first week back, but you don't listen to me. You're stubborn, but a fighter, I'll give you that."

"A fighter that's getting her butt kicked by a cold now too." She sniffed at the barrier in her nose. "Every time I swallow, my ears crack."

"Oh, Kathy, you know how vulnerable we are working here and you're not up to full strength. Why don't you have one of the doctors look you over before you go home?"

"No, I'll be fine."

"If it is a cold then they can give you something before it gets any worse. That is unless you want to spend your two days off in misery?"

Kathy shook her head. "My body will fight it off."

"You see? As stubborn as a mule."

"So I've been told," she said, knowing her true ailment, the one she tried to bury deep down inside was a severe form of depression topped off with fatigue. Maybe Jaiden's company would distract her enough that she might forget how empty her life had become since the tragic event that broke her spine in two and killed her husband.

"If you change your mind," Claire said, ripping her from her thoughts. "Maybe you'll get lucky and get that new doctor everyone is talking about."

Kathy laughed. "Oh, come on. Everyone is talking about this guy. He can't be that good looking."

Claire raised her eyebrows and grinned. "You say that now, but after you see him, you'll change your mind. I guarantee that."

Kathy laughed again and grabbed her pocketbook off the desk. "You really need to get out more."

"Tall, dark and handsome."

"I'm a long way away from caring about that," Kathy said, and knocked on Claire's desktop. "I'll see you Monday night."

Kathy walked to the elevator lobby and pressed the down button. She waited for one of four cars to come for her, and with a loud *ding*, doors behind her slid open and she stepped inside.

When she arrived at the ground floor, she tried to step out of the elevator but a tall, elegantly thin young woman with a face like a porcelain doll stood in her way. The woman held onto a lush bouquet of flowers.

"Excuse me," the porcelain faced woman said, her voice like the strum of a finely tuned harp. She stepped aside and allowed Kathy room to pass.

Kathy smiled and refrained from telling the woman that it was too late for visitors. "Thank you," she said instead and stepped out of the elevator.

"Lady Kathy?"

Kathy turned and looked at the woman.

"We know your life has been hard and you need to know that things will become harder before you are rewarded."

Kathy looked behind herself and expected to see someone else standing there. But they were alone.

"In the end," the porcelain-faced woman said, "your prize will be great. You will learn to love again without restriction."

Kathy stared for a second, confusion twirling all around her. "Are you talking to me?"

"You know that I am. And try to remember that in the coming days your suffering is recognized and your character is being tested."

The porcelain-faced woman stepped into the elevator and pressed the button. "There will be a man coming to you," she said. "You need to be strong for him, so much depends on it."

Kathy watched the elevator doors slide closed.

"That was weird," she said, and shook her head.

She exited the hospital with the strange woman's words resonating in her head over and over again. She walked through the poorly lit parking garage and hurried towards her reserved parking spot. The idea of being tested and having a man come to her seemed ridiculous. The wind carried a bitter chill that penetrated her thin sweater and she shivered at its bite.

Tap. Tap. Tap.

Kathy turned towards the sound and searched the surrounding area.

Tap. Tap. Tap.

It was elusive but seemed as though it was purposely following and stopping to avoid detection.

Maybe it was Ted and he was going to settle the score with Megan by coming after her.

"No," Kathy said. "That's crazy thinking. He's long gone, probably in a gutter somewhere in a drunken stupor."

Besides, things like that only happened to weak people and Kathy wasn't weak. The doctors told her that the day she began to walk again.

"I'm sorry, but were you talking to me?"

Kathy screamed and jumped back. A tall, slender man with salt and pepper hair looked back at her. His tanned face had no imperfections and his eyes were wide with his question.

"Oh my god," Kathy said, and placed a hand over her pounding heart. "I thought I heard someone, but didn't see anyone. I was talking to myself, and when you spoke it really startled me. I didn't know you were there."

"Sound carries around in this cement structure and it's hard to tell where it's coming from," he said, his smile warming.

Kathy extended her hand while she eyed the man's white smock. He had a picture identification tag clipped to his breast pocket.

"Hello Doctor Williams," she said. "I'm Kathy Odonnell and I work in the recovery ward. I've heard a lot about you."

The doctor kept his hands at his sides.

"And I know a lot about you, too. I can only wonder how you can work in recovery when you haven't quite recovered yourself," he said.

Kathy furrowed her brows. "Excuse me?"

"You'll never get past what happened to him."

"What are you talking about?"

"Rocco. I know he died not too long ago and the memory of that must be fresh. Terribly painful, I'm sure that it hurts deep down into your soul. It happened on your wedding night, did it not?"

Her adrenaline soared. "Who are you?"

"You broke your back and the doctors said you would never walk again."

"How do you know this?"

He laughed. "Let's just say that I know everything. All of your wants and fears. Your past and future."

She stared at him stone-faced and confused, her anger making her forget her permanent discomfort.

"I don't like the look you're giving me," he said. "You should be happy. You're alive and a walking miracle. The last two years of your life has been filled with so much tragedy that even I feel bad for you."

The doctor looked left, right and then back at Kathy.

"And I've come here to give you a chance. I know you really don't know what that means, but I assure you that I don't offer many of them. Tonight when you get home, don't take the man in rags into your home. His injuries are none of your concern."

"What man?"

"You should be quiet and listen to what I have to say. My time is valuable and to give it to a stack of bones seems so wasteful. The decisions you make in the next few hours are going to determine how much more difficult your life is going to become. Being human is what makes you flawed and I believe my efforts here are for nothing. But I don't mind that you're going to force my hand because what will follow is what I'm really good at."

"Excuse me, but are you threatening me?"

"Something as beautiful as you shouldn't have to suffer the way your husband did. Now that would be a pity."

Kathy's mouth opened but there were no words. She watched the doctor simply turn around and walk away.

"I remember how terrible those last few moments were for the both of you," he said, his voice gradually fading into the distance. "But you are the one that has to live with the memory of him being trapped inside that wreckage, just beyond your reach."

She forgot about the chill that continued to nibble at her skin. Lost within the doctor's ominous warning, the wind howled and the intensity of it pulled her from her reverie.

Fear entered her body and iced her blood. She motioned to run but the pain in her lower back returned with a vengeance. Limping to her car, she got into the driver's seat, pulled the door closed and locked them.

"What the hell was that all about?" she said, and with trembling hands she started the engine and drove off.

CHAPTER 3

DEEP, DARK STAIRWELL

Friday, October 14th, 1:47 am

Kathy watched the rearview mirror with an unwavering intensity. Traffic was light and her ability to spot anyone that might have followed her would have been easy to see.

The night offered two strange encounters that left her on edge. The first was the woman inside the hospital. Though her words were ominous, she seemed genuinely concerned and gentle. On the other hand, the doctor was scary and said things that were hurtful and perplexing.

"How could he know those things?"

Kathy circled her apartment complex one last time before she was satisfied that she wasn't being followed. Pulling into a parking spot located across the street, the four-story brick building she lived in looked like a fort and she desired its protection.

Hurrying out of the car and bounding the steep cement steps two steps at a time, the threat of back pain meant nothing compared to her dread. She desired the security the building would provide and help protect her from the strange people that suddenly inserted themselves into her life.

"Hey lady!"

The words were faint, but Kathy heard them and paused at the top step and listened.

"I need your help."

Kathy grabbed the cold iron handrail and peered over the side. The wind nipped at her flesh and she searched the impossible darkness below.

"Did someone just say they needed my help?" she said into the black.

The basement apartments had remained unoccupied since she moved in just after being released from the hospital. She never returned to the home she shared with her husband again. The memories of trying to start a life together were too painful and she reasoned that the change of scenery might help her during the healing process.

From what Kathy knew, the basement area was being converted from a storage area into apartments, but the tough economy halted the construction.

"Hello? Are you hurt?" she said, and her teeth chattered.

A grunt followed by the sound of something being dragged across the floor held her attention.

As of late, the stairwell had become a hangout for the local kids. But this night, the chill in the air was too bitter and the desperate tone of the voice made her believe whoever was down there was in trouble and in need of her help.

"I can hear you down there," she said, her voice growing louder. "I'm going to call the police."

Curiosity kept her still, but a sudden and intense sensation of danger told her to flee while she still had the chance. It was a similar feeling she had when the doctor started saying things about her husband he should never have known.

She resisted the urge and kept her focus on the stairwell below. Walking down a few steps, she remained cautious but determined to see what had conflicted her so, but it was no use. The darkness was too thick for her eyes to penetrate and it was too frightening and dangerous for her to get any closer.

"I'm leaving now," she said, and waited a few moments. No further sounds could be heard. The tremors in her jaw seized and a sudden, powerful chill shook her body as if it were an encouraging shove to move on. She rubbed her hands together and folded her arms across her chest.

"Just debris being blown around by the wind," she convinced herself, and started up the stairs again. When she reached the top step, she unlocked the lobby door and pulled it open.

"Please, I need your help," a man said, but this time his voice was loud and near and somewhere close behind her.

Kathy gasped and turned to see a big man standing at the bottom of the stairs. He too was tall and slender. Tattered clothes hung off of his bruised and blood-smeared body. He swayed and his eyes were wide and desperate. She rushed to his side and struggled against her back pain to hold him upright.

Helping him sit on the bottom step, she encouraged him to lean against the iron handrail.

"Remain as still as you can," she said.

She knelt in front of him and looked him over. Lacerations on his arms, face and head trickled blood and told a horrible story. Massive swelling closed an eye and his lips were puffy.

"I need to call for help," she said and stood. But the man reached out and latched onto her arm.

"No," he said, and grimaced. He coughed and spit blood onto the walkway. "You cannot under any circumstance call an ambulance or the police. If you do, you will endanger me even further."

Kathy could have easily pulled away from his grasp, but she didn't want to risk making him fall.

"My name is Sam," he said, and released Kathy's arm. He wiped his mouth with the back of his hand. "It's not as bad as it looks."

The thought of digging her cell phone out of her pocketbook wrestled with her desire to know what had happened to him and kept her quiet and curious.

"Please," he said. "You have to get me inside. I know they're after me, and if they find me, they'll kill me and make you pay for ever having laid eyes on me."

Kathy looked over her shoulder. "Who?"

"People that will believe you know everything. And if they believe that, they won't allow you to live."

Kathy looked down the street both ways. It was empty and quiet—that is, everything but the whipping wind.

"Whoever they are, I think you got away from them," she said.

Sam laughed, grabbed his side and scowled.

"You don't understand," he said, out of breath. "And right now, I don't have the time to explain. You wouldn't be able to see them even if they were near."

His words were unbelievable and so were all of the events that transpired the moment she got off of work.

"Please," he said, and tried to stand on his own. "This all sounds crazy, I know, but I'll explain everything. But before I do, you have to get me off the streets."

Kathy couldn't ignore the desperateness in Sam's voice and she knew he didn't pose a threat in the condition he was in. She pulled him to his feet and her back filled her body with pain. Fighting through it and moving his arm around her shoulders, she walked him into the apartment building. Having to pause at a second flight of stairs, she heaved a sigh and rested a moment. "I know you're injuries are bad, but I need you to help me. You're heavy."

Step by step they moved closer until they reached the landing and stood in front of Kathy's door. They leaned on each other so she could gather her keys to unlock the deadbolt and handle. The hinges whined as the door swung open. The furniture in the dark living room looked like big things crouching.

Kathy used the slivers of light that penetrated the window shades to navigate the long hallway that dead-ended at a guest bedroom. She eased Sam into the bed, pulled the frayed, blood-soaked shirt off of his back, and encouraged him to lean against the headboard.

Once Sam was balanced, she went into the bathroom and gathered gauze wrap, cotton balls, medical tape, peroxide, and Tylenol with codeine. Returning to the spare bedroom, she sat next to Sam.

Kathy gathered a handful of cotton balls and doused them with peroxide. She dabbed the wounds and worked slow, cleaning the caked blood and dirt that embedded itself into the sliced flesh.

Sam grunted in discomfort and Kathy continued to work undaunted.

"You should consider seeing a doctor," she said. "The abrasions I'll be able to take care of, but the internal injuries and the head trauma needs to be evaluated and treated by an actual doctor in a hospital. I can take you there and get the best doctor to look at you."

"No doctors," he said. "I'm sure they've infiltrated the hospitals already. I need to wait until morning before I chance moving."

Kathy was reminded of the porcelain-faced woman and the encounter she had with the doctor inside the parking garage but thought it better if she didn't mention it. "Who are these people that are after you?"

"No one good," he said. "Let's leave it at that for the time being, okay? I'm sorry, it hurts to talk."

She finished cleaning the wounds without another word and covered them with bandages.

"I need you to lie down," she said, and helped Sam get underneath the blankets. "I'll be back in a moment to check on you."

She returned the first aid products to the medicine cabinet. When she returned to Sam, he was fast asleep. In that moment, she couldn't help but notice how beautiful he was. Even beneath the swelling and bandages, she could see something attractive and irresistible about him. His cheekbones, jaw line and complexion were so perfect that he seemed fake—almost as if he was cast from a mold.

She eased herself onto the foot of the bed and moved with care so she didn't wake him. Collapsing to her back, she mindlessly watched the twisting light from vehicles that passed dance on the ceiling. The merciless pain drained out of her body and she planned to lie there for a little while. Maybe she would stay long enough to keep watch over Sam and enjoy the pain-free moment.

Different scenarios played out in her mind as she tried to figure out whom or what could have beaten Sam and had him frightened enough to hide in a stairwell. Maybe he had ties to a gang or messed with another man's woman? Maybe the people that came to her in the hospital had a case of mistaken identity.

She knew any of these things were possible. She also knew drug addicts didn't always look disheveled and desperate. All too often she would get a reminder of that at work. And in her heart, she didn't believe

Sam would have much trouble enticing a woman, married or otherwise.

"No," she said, and shook her head.

It couldn't have been one man that did all that damage to him. He appeared to be in great shape and seemed much too big for one man to handle.

Kathy had always liked bigger men. She felt more secure in their arms, wrapped in their tight grasp. Something about having to look up at them made her feel more feminine. Sam looked to be about the same size as Rocco, and she always felt he was the perfect size for her. Big and huggable like a teddy bear, the thought of him made Kathy smile. God how she wished it were him lying in the bed beside her.

Her mind began to wander and play out desires she would normally try and repress. The last few years of her life didn't allow such thoughts. Recovery and horrible memories topped off with nightmares of the accident was all she could think of. Besides, her strict religious upbringing always said it was sinful to knowingly lust. She defied such weaknesses and hardly ever gave in to such temptation.

But this night, she would let it slide because she was sure no one was listening to her private thoughts in the small room out of this great big world.

She pictured herself and Sam in the back seat of a limousine, sitting close, sipping bubbling wine. Their bliss reflected in fanciful colors of swirling bar lights. Glimmering eyes and sparkling stones on their fingers represented a promise that said so much more than a succession of three words ever could. It was an unwavering representation of their love, commitment and their promise of staying together through all of life's challenges, no matter what.

The vehicle they occupied eased to a gradual stop and moments later the door was opened by the driver. Sam stepped out first. The driver stepped forward, took Kathy by the hand and helped her out of the limousine. She stared at him knowing she'd seen him before, feeling as though she'd known him her entire life.

Paying her no mind, the driver passed her off to Sam.

"You look beautiful," Sam said, and twirled her lovingly, stealing her attention. Kathy batted her eyelashes that felt overly long and thick with makeup and she thanked Sam for being so cordial. This day was as perfect as it was meant to be. Sam bowed and offered Kathy an arm. Kathy took his arm and began walking hand-in-hand with him on a trail carved by humans inside a nature preserve.

She glanced back curiously at the limousine and its driver. The vehicle's exterior was smashed like it had been in a violent accident. Fluids spilled into the street, and unexplainably, the driver was buffing the creased hood with care. She paused and shivered unknowingly at the discovery and Sam gently tugged her hand.

"Never mind that. Come," he said, and her legs began to walk and her eyes moved away from the vehicle.

The wind was blowing about the preserve, gently rocking the treetops back and forth, rustling the foliage on the ground and pulling the browning leaves off of their branches. The slow moving brook beside the trail trickled through a sinuous rivulet. Birds chirped wildly; the foreign language of their call was like music to the ears.

The two continued to walk the path and explore its beauty. Releasing hands and wrapping arms around each other's waists, she could feel her love for Sam, his strength, and the radiance of his body heat. She offered him a smile, although it meant so much more. Taking in a deep breath, she sucked in the clean warm air and slowly released it in full appreciation of life.

She moved her focus to the sunlight breaking through the trees above.

Intoxicating.

Kathy looked at Sam and he to her. They exchanged smiles, and then a kiss. Content, she rested her head on his broad shoulder and involuntarily panned the milieu.

In an instant, the backdrop of the preserve morphed. The surrounding cluster of trees on all sides repressed all penetrating beams of sunlight, and above, the tree branches meshed together and formed a tight impenetrable barrier. The darkness appeared to be coming alive and it spread at an alarmingly fast pace. Before Kathy could alert Sam, the entire forest surrounded them in a dull grayness that felt heavy.

In the dim darkness, just on the forest's edge, movement caught Kathy's attention. The feeling of love rushed out of her and was replaced by inexplicable terror that brought forth sheer panic. She wanted to run, but needed to see. Many eyes that were big and orange stared at her and Sam. They watched their every move from within the shadows of the forest. How strange this all felt to her. It was all so real, but knowingly forged. She looked at Sam for protection, but he was seemingly oblivious, continuing to drag her along the path, consumed with the thought of love.

She tried to say something, anything at all, but had no voice to utter a single word. She tried to point out the eyes dwelling within the forest, but her arms were too heavy to lift. She wanted to whimper but whispered the words, "I love you" instead.

"Of course you do," Sam said, and she could smell the wonderful fragrance of his breath. "And I love you too. That is why I've brought you here. I want you to meet Belial."

Is that all?

Kathy suddenly felt relaxed. She would do anything to please Sam, even brave a blackened forest filled with goblins.

Sam continued to escort Kathy, leading her off the path and to the edge of the forest where the creatures with the orange eyes continued to gather and frenzy with excitement.

"Belial?" Sam called forth, and Kathy was again paralyzed with fear. The nearness of the frothing beasts was like death walking beside her. She struggled to breathe and to maintain control over herself.

"Belial?" Sam said again, this time his voice growing louder. "I've brought my contribution to you."

All sets of the orange eyes backed away, and one pair of red eyes approached. The eyes settled at the edge of darkness and narrowed as they studied Kathy unreservedly.

"Contribution?" Kathy managed to say and looked at Sam with confusion.

Sam smiled, his teeth shining in the darkness and his eyes twinkled as he looked at Kathy. "Yes, for the love we feel. For our love. You'd be willing to do anything for the love we share, wouldn't you?"

Sam looked back at the frightening set of eyes eerily covered by the living curtain of shadows, and looked upon them with a consuming love. Maybe the love he was feeling, Kathy realized, was for Belial and the darkness and not for her.

Kathy returned her attention to those red eyes—not because she wanted to, rather, as if she was being commanded to do so by a muted voice that couldn't be ignored.

"Leave here, Sardurvial," the beast said from within the forest. But stranger still, his voice was beautiful.

"Have fun, my love," Sam said, and turned and walked away.

Kathy stood alone, quivering before the living shadow, fearful for her life. The beast within the shadow growled its warning. The resounding tone he produced was low and domineering and standoffish. In the wake of its might, Kathy weakened and dropped to her knees but she was unable to pry her eyes from the penetrating stare and their mesmerizing blood red glow. She was paralyzed, helpless and vulnerable.

The beast lunged forward. Kathy saw it coming and closed her eyes and braced herself for impact. It didn't come, but she could feel the heat of the beast's breath drumming off the back of her neck. She didn't want to look at it but felt like she needed to.

Slowly opening her eyes, she turned and stared in awe at the attractive man who looked like Doctor William. But the anger he wore disguised his beauty. How could someone so handsome be so ugly? He was tainted with hatred and made no attempt to hide the fact.

The man roared like a feral animal in Kathy's face. She sat up and gasped for air. The heavy blankets she'd placed on Sam had somehow ended on top of her too. She was soaked with sweat and her heart pounded. To her relief, it was all just a bad dream.

Being careful not to wake Sam, Kathy shimmied out of the bed and went into the bathroom to wash her face.

Exiting the bathroom, by use of the moonlight shining through the window inside the living room, she walked directly to her bedroom. The digital clock on her desk read 4:30 am.

Letting out a ferocious yawn and stretching her arms wide, Kathy pulled the blankets on her bed to the side. Unzipping the back of her nurse's uniform, she kicked off her shoes, removed her stockings, and slipped off her outfit and slid into bed.

Pulling the covers over her body, she shifted until she found comfort on her side. Striving for nothing other than sleep, Kathy failed to notice the man that blended with the shadows of the night and sat in her reading chair in the corner of the room.

The shrouded figure kept his head down. He didn't plan on lifting it until he was sure Kathy was sound asleep. And once she was, he would remain in the seat with his red eyes aglow, watching her in silence and contemplating her future—the consequences for aiding an apostate that foolishly chose to stand against his cause and hide among the people.

CHAPTER 4

THE DAMN PEOPLE
11,000 BC

Sitting atop scattered boulders beside a beautiful blue lake, five great friends, Aramus, Sardurvial, Jesseth, Ishmael, and Abraham found themselves in deep discussion. Deliberating a future that looked uncertain, worry aggrieved them all.

In a nearby cluster of trees Belial hid behind the undergrowth and settled in as quietly as possible.

"I just can't believe it though," Aramus said, and from where Belial kept cover, he had no trouble hearing the words. "When we were first told about the idea of the creation of man, I didn't think He would take the project so seriously. I thought for sure the silly notion would pass and He would move on in His desire to create. But now that He has shaped them, it's as though His care is strictly for the people. I'm beginning to worry for us!"

Everyone around grumbled their agreement.

"It seems He spends every waking moment worrying about them and their meaningless lives," Aramus continued. "I wonder, have any of you seen the way the people behave? They're vile beasts that turn against one another! It seems as though their imperfections have Him bewildered and so concerned that He doesn't have any care for us."

"Aye, I've seen the people and you're right Aramus," Abraham said. "They behave like animals. The only thing He's worried about is how He's going to save them from their destructive ways. I hate to say it, but for some reason I feel as though we mean nothing to Him."

"Agreed," Sardurvial said and tossed a stone into the lake. The water rippled. "We were pushed aside as if we meant nothing, moved away for something that sinks to the bottom like that rock."

"I'm terrified of what is to come," Ishmael said, his face full of worry. "Do you think the people were meant to take our place? Do you think our blind obedience has somehow caused this?"

"Our obedience has nothing to do with the way we're being treated," Aramus said.

"It has plenty to do with it, can't you see?" Ishmael said. "Maybe He sees our willingness to obey as . . . I don't know, as boring? He just says and we do without objection or question. The people don't. They ignore His commandments without regard and blatantly defy His word. I don't understand why He even needed to create them. They were made imperfect. They are like spoiled food that should be thrown in the trash and remade, and yet, they enamor Him and He desperately searches for a way to offer them salvation. Have you ever thought why we aren't forgiven if we disobey?"

Each looked to the other and no one dared to answer the question.

Rustling in nearby trees stole their attention. Belial emerged from the brush tightlipped and his chin down. As he moved before them, he glanced at each.

"Haven't I told you this would happen?" Belial said, his tone reprimanding and confident. "I tried to warn you all, but you just wouldn't listen! I felt like a fool after I told you I suspected His changes and you looked at me as if I had gone mad! Madness is that all of you failed to see what I saw so long ago!"

He paced, seething with anger.

"Those damn people! How many of you chastised me for my telling you this?"

Belial stared at each of them, his eyes bulging and untamed. None looked to meet his reproachful gaze.

"As the days go by," Belial said, suddenly calm. "You will all see that He is only going to get more and more distant and I'm afraid things are only going to get worse. I think our welcome here may be overstayed."

Belial sighed.

"I can only wonder why you couldn't see this the day I tried to tell you," he muttered. He clasped his hands behind his back, dropped his chin, and steadied his focus on the small group.

"I know I can lead you and any other who would be willing to follow me to a greater glory."

He slowly raised his eyes and looked out on the lake.

"Although we are surrounded by perfect beauty, we shouldn't be lulled into blind obedience. We should consider moving before we are shamefully ousted. We can make preparations to build our own society among the people. There we can rule and make of the people what we wish without having to justify their imperfections like He does. We can exploit their weaknesses. They will give to us what we desire and they will live by the rules we set. I will confront God Himself and tell Him this!"

Silence blanketed the group as they considered his words. Belial looked at his colleagues expectantly.

"But, Belial, we cannot look to stand against God!" Ishmael said. "He is our creator and He is far too powerful. It would be like playing with fire."

Belial tittered in defiance.

"He wants us to believe that we are helpless in our fight, but I know better. I've discovered a secret hidden inside His sleeping chambers. This object, if we were able to get our hands on, would change our destinies forevermore."

"Aye, Belial, this thing you speak of, what is it?" Abraham said.

Jesseth hopped off his rock and fixed Abraham with a hardened stare. "It doesn't matter what it is, Abraham. Belial is crazy for thinking we could ever enter God's sleeping chambers and steal from Him. If we were to get caught, do you have any idea what the punishment would be? I dare not think it!" Jesseth returned to his rock, and settled. "Never has anyone been so brazen to even think such a thing let alone seriously consider following through with it."

Belial shook his head knowingly. "You're right, Jesseth, and very smart for thinking that way, too. But everything you just said I've already realized and I'm willing to face punishment alone if I'm caught in my attempt to take what God is hiding. After I gain possession of this timeless artifact, I will return to you. Then and only then will I ask you to follow me in my stand against God. And when that time comes, the choice for you to join me will be offered. But given the time that will pass between now and then, I doubt you'll reject me. I say this because I can only see God getting more and more distant from us. Our need to feel a sense of love and family will be great and our options limited. He will force our hand."

Belial turned and began to walk towards the forest he emerged from. "Oh," he said. "Pass the word about what I've said, but only to those you trust enough with your lives. If He hears we're conspiring, He may send forth His wrath. Understand, we are not prepared to face such fury." He paused and looked over his shoulder. "At least not yet."

CHAPTER 5

A CHILD'S IMAGINATION

Friday, October 14th, 11:35 pm

Jaiden Michael had been tucked into bed over three and a half hours ago. He found himself wide-awake, alone and very afraid of the thing that occupied the darkness around him.

Every night he had frightening encounters with the monster and he couldn't get the nerve to take a stand against it. He wanted his father, but would settle for his mother this night even though she was the one that got him into this mess. Without his father being home, he didn't have anyone to check beneath his bed and look in his closet to scare the creature away.

His anxiety over having to face it night after night increased but he didn't dare tell his mother. She would scold him and deny his claims. The only thing he could do was keep his eyes trained on the closet door for hours and hope it didn't come. But it lived in there, this beast, and it would come again this night as it did every night before. After an hour of intense watching, he had become so tired he couldn't fight the need to sleep.

Something that was loud and clumsy had awoken him. And yet it was smart enough not to make noise loud enough to gain his mother's attention.

Jaiden's head buzzed from sleep and he listened to things inside of his closet crash to the ground. A low ferocious growl directed at him came blasting through the small space between the closet door and floor.

Pressed firmly in the bed, Jaiden's fear trembled his body as he listened to the closet door whine as it slowly swung open. He pulled the covers to the bridge of his nose and searched the dark corner with widened eyes. He couldn't see anything and his panic increased.

"Mommy," he whispered, very afraid, unconcerned about her judgment. The sound of his heart pounding rattled his ribcage and filled his ears.

He could hear the monster as it moved around freely, taunting him. It began to probe the clutter on the underside of his bed and the beast moved slowly, testing the limits of his fear.

He tried to scream for his mother but only managed a dull croak. The idea of running out of the room and jumping into his mother's bed where he could tell her about the monster was quickly dismissed when he tried to move. His legs felt like unmovable stone pillars.

The light.

He looked at the lamp on the night table beside his bed and it seemed so far away. There was no question that the light would scare the beast off because it would burn its skin. But he also knew if he were to reach out for the light the beast would get him and drag him into the deep dark corner it hid in and nobody would be able to find him.

The dread that swirled inside of Jaiden and the overwhelming sense of panic controlled him. It kept him from taking that leap from his bed and making a run for it and prevented him from reaching out past his bed to turn on the light.

So he did the only thing he could. He remained perfectly still and used his covers as a shield and hugged his pillow, braving the beast.

Several more hours had passed and Jaiden continued to remain still. The entire time he listened to thumping sounds coming from the underside of his bed. The beast sounded big and he pictured it looking something like an alligator. Or maybe it was lizard like.

Whatever it looked like, it had a hard time maneuvering around the clutter. A few times he could feel it slam the underside of his bed and jiggle the mattress.

Worry soon exhausted his young mind and he drifted into sleep.

Saturday, October 15, 9:50 am

Jaiden batted his heavy eyes as he emerged from sleep. His midnight encounter with the beast was still fresh on his mind. He sat up and looked at the closet with uncertainty.

Now that it was morning, he knew whatever it was that came for him was long gone and it was kind enough to close the closet door on its way out.

Jaiden hopped out of bed and approached the closet with caution. Apprehensive and nervous that the beast might still be lurking within the confined darkness, he inched towards the closet door. Being careful not to make contact with the wooden slats, he peered inside and struggled to get a glimpse of what hid within. He strained his eyes and shifted his position, but it was of no use. The darkness kept all of its secrets well hidden.

The door to Jaiden's bedroom swung open and his mother hurried inside, carrying a neatly folded stack of clothes within the cusp of her arms. Jaiden hooted and stumbled backwards, tripping over a pair of shoes and he fell down with a heavy thump.

Megan placed the stack of clothes on Jaiden's bed and rushed to her son's side.

"Are you okay, Jaiden? You've got to be more careful."

Before Megan could help her son up, he quickly hopped to his feet and moved the sneakers he'd left in the middle of the floor to the side.

"I'm fine mom," he said, rubbing his backside. "You should have knocked. What if I was getting dressed?"

He turned away.

"You're right, I'm sorry," she said. She went to console him and when she drew near, she saw him eyeballing the closet door.

"Did you have another bad dream?" she said, and knelt in front of him. She took his hands and pulled him close, hugging him.

"It wasn't a dream," Jaiden muttered, unwilling to return the gesture. "It came from—"

"The closet?" Megan said, and sighed. She stood up and walked to the closet door. "We've gone through this a million times, Jaiden. There is nothing in your closet. Not now and not in the middle of the night!"

She yanked the closet door open and Jaiden retreated. Megan looked inside the neat full-sized closet and paused a moment before she looked back at her son.

"You see? There's nothing in here but your clothes."

Jaiden walked to the bed and sat. His eyes wandered aimlessly, trying desperately to shelter the distress within. She couldn't possibly understand him or what he was going through. It was obvious she thought he was making it all up and he felt disheartened to know that.

"I'm not making any of this up," he said. "I know what I heard."

"I don't think you're making it up," she said. "Look, when I was a child, I had dolls on top of my dresser. I swore they were watching me, waiting for me to fall asleep. I'd stay awake for hours watching them, swearing I'd see them move."

"This isn't helping, mom."

"No," she said. "I'm not very good at this and that wasn't a good thing for me to say. I'm sorry."

"It's okay mom."

"But those dolls that I thought were watching me were really only in my imagination. Maybe you think this is happening because your father isn't home right now."

"Mom . . ."

"No, it's okay. I understand that. Maybe tonight things will get better for you," she said.

He sighed.

"I just want you to be happy."

"I am happy."

"Not as happy as you deserve to be."

"Is dad coming home soon?"

"Whether he is or not doesn't change the fact that there are no such things as monsters. And even if there were, you know I'd protect you from them no matter how big and scary they were."

Jaiden didn't respond and Megan rubbed his head.

"You're a good kid Jaiden. Don't you ever think anything different. I'm going to start on breakfast," she said. "You have a few minutes before you have to come down and eat."

She exited the room and closed the door behind her.

Jaiden sat quietly for a moment, staring into his closet. He tried to figure out where the monster went to hide when his mother looked for it. There weren't any holes in the wall or ceiling and he was sure there weren't any hidden trap doors. He needed to check again, but this time more thoroughly while he had daylight.

Inching towards the closet, apprehension tickled his nerves and he could feel the beast's nearness again. He slammed the closet door shut, sprinted out of his room, hurdled the steps and slowed his pace as he came into the kitchen. With a casual smile aimed at his mother, he took a seat at the table.

Megan's slender body was wrapped in a flowered apron that clung to her shapely hips. She gracefully tiptoed across the kitchen floor and gave her son another kiss. Jaiden wiped the wet kiss away and hugged his mother back. Megan squeezed him tight and returned her attention to the stovetop. Frying eggs and four strips of bacon that hissed and crackled in a pool of boiling grease, the aroma was wonderful and compelled her stomach to growl in anticipation.

"I'd like to go food shopping today."

Jaiden nodded. "Okay mom."

"Why don't you take a shower after you eat your breakfast," she said. "Put on your denim jeans and wear that heavy wool sweater your aunt got you last year. It's colder outside today than it was yesterday and yesterday you told me you were cold."

"Am I still going to Aunt Kathy's house tonight?" Jaiden said.

"That's why I want you to wear that sweater. She'll be thrilled to see you wearing it."

"Awesome!" Jaiden said and pumped his fist.

Megan shut off the burner underneath the frying pan and she carried the hot skillet over to Jaiden's plate. She scraped eggs on one half of the plate and returned the skillet to the range top. Fetching the bacon, she placed them on Jaiden's plate next to the eggs and hurried to the fridge and poured a glass of orange juice and set it on the table next to the plate.

"I'm going back upstairs to put away the laundry," she said. "I'd like you to try to finish your breakfast by the time I come back down so we can start our day."

Jaiden concentrated his gaze on the cooling mound of yellow mush on the plate before him, and nodded his head in agreement as he shoveled a heaping forkful of eggs into his mouth.

Megan strolled out of the room, climbed the stairs and went directly into Jaiden's bedroom. She opened the blinds to allow the sunlight to enter the room and stood in the penetrating shaft of light to embrace its warmth.

Returning to the task at hand, she gathered the stack of laundry she'd left on the bed and moved it to the top of the bureau. Separating the clothing and placing each piece inside the corresponding drawer, Megan came to a pair of slacks and a button down shirt that was to be used for special occasions. She walked to the closet and opened the door, half imagining the monster would be there and ready to strike. Of course she found nothing out of the ordinary and took a step inside the closet.

Tugging the chain that dangled in the center of the closet, she turned on the light. She rearranged some of the clothes on the rack and grabbed an empty hanger and placed the shirt on it. Hanging it back up, she took a second hanger and placed the pants on it and hung that up.

The room outside of the closet quickly lost its light as if something massive blocked the sun. But Megan continued to work on the clothes, encased in the overhead light, oblivious to what was happening behind her.

Finished, Megan turned off the light and the sudden blackness stilled her feet.

A red glowing speck of light that appeared in the distance held her attention. She focused on the source and felt a sudden sense of comfort and watched it with hope. As the speck continued to grow, it gently split into two and her hope doubled.

"Eyes," Megan whispered. "That is the eyes of something wicked."

Strangely, she didn't fear the eyes or the wickedness within them. Instead, she welcomed them, awaited their coming with expectation and fidelity. She couldn't understand why, but she did. She never saw anything like this before and knew she should fear them. But now, in this moment, she started to walk towards them, obeying the deaf order to approach.

Once she stood before them, she stared in awe and reached to touch the face that remained hidden in the obscurity that surrounded them. On contact she knew the face she felt was a man's. His skin was soft and his lips were parted ever so slightly in a satisfied smirk.

She liked what she felt too, was turned on by it, and wanted to see what it looked like in the light. She felt her way to his hand and placed hers in his.

"Take me to the light," she said. "I want to see you."

Megan was led to the center of the closet in silence; the dangling chain from the light skimmed the top of her head. She reached up and gave it a tug.

A beautiful man stood beside her. At first sight, she fell in love.

She stared at him and acknowledged that he was everything she thought he would be, and maybe even more. His eyes were majestic, and they encouraged her to see the rest of him.

His chest was bare and looked as though it had been sculpted from fine stone. Her eyes moved down slowly, studying every inch of him. The definition and ripples of his pectorals and abs were flawless.

A smile parted her lips and she worked her hands downwards. She hadn't seen or touched another man since her early days of high school. Megan always remained faithful to Ted, even through the times of intense emotional and physical abuse. But this wasn't high school anymore, and for this moment, she was done with Ted. She was pulsing with desire and saw the lust in his eyes and how they screamed for her. Her love was turning to lust and she couldn't resist it. Megan allowed her eyes to wander, and they eventually found her hands and what they held.

She stared at it in disbelief. She twirled it and tugged on it and the beautiful man swayed with her movement. The extremity was connected to him but around the backside of his body.

"Oh my—"

The man covered her mouth. "Shh," he said. "You don't want your son to hear this."

She let go of his tail and wiped her hands on her thighs. Sickened by her unclean thoughts and by this man's deformed body, she wanted to run away. But she couldn't.

She looked at what she lusted for and gagged violently.

The beautiful man giggled without sound. His shoulders bounced and his broad smile expressed sheer delight that filled her with terror. In that instant, the comfort of his presence was now gone. The fear she should have felt earlier now swept over her and snuffed any opportunity she had to flee.

The beast that stood before Megan could sense the dread growing inside her as he circled and appraised her body, but never her soul. He knew he would have that soon enough. Not by force, but rather, by her own bad judgment with a dash of his influence.

She would be perfect. There was no question about that because his planning was always ingenious. He paused before her, and slowly reached his hand out and tugged on the chain.

Click.

The closet went dark.

CHAPTER 6

SEPARATING DREAMS FROM REALITY

Saturday, October 15th, 9:30 am

The alarm on the nightstand beeped diligently and pried Kathy out of her deep sleep. Pounding the snooze button with a sigh, she rolled to her side. Every inch of her body ached.

Pulling the blanket over her head, she attempted to hide from the sunlight that penetrated the shades and forget about her ailments for a little while. Within minutes, she was drifting back to sleep as if she'd never been disturbed.

Deet! Deet! Deet!

She rolled over with a groan and shut the alarm off. The cold that clogged her head seemed to have worsened and her eyes were sore and felt like someone had applied a thick layer of paste on them while she slept. Picking at the dried rheum with her pointer finger and thumb, an emerging memory shifted her focus to the vivid details of her journey through the beautiful forest that quickly turned ugly. The smashed limousine and the image of her deceased husband being the driver made her sit up. A tremble that was in the pit of her belly threatened to rush up her throat and explode in a fitful wail. She repressed her sorrow and tried to honor Rocco's dying wish:

"Don't you ever think of me like this and always remember our good days together."

She reflected on a moment in time filled with bliss and her joy embattled her despair. Turning her focus to a picture of her and Rocco wrapped tight in a warm embrace sat on the night table, angled so she could look at him and he at her while she slept. The picture was taken when it was a much happier time for them. That was what she needed to remember because that was what he wanted.

She rolled over with her thoughts turning to the man named Sam that she discovered outside her apartment last night. Uncertain if the event was real or not, the telephone beside her bed clamored to life. It startled her and the sound penetrated the stuffiness in her ears and rattled her head. Burying her face in the mound of pillows, it muffled the piercing noise.

"Damn cold had to wait until I was off. Just my luck."

The answering machine picked up the call and her first guess was that it was Claire. She needed her to come into work because there was no one else available to come in so she waited and listened.

"Hello, Kathy? It's me, are you there?" Megan said into the machine. "Pick up!"

Kathy reached for the telephone. "Hello, Megan."

"Hi, Kathy," Megan said. "I'm sorry, I hope I didn't wake you."

"No," she said. "My alarm got me before you did."

"Are you okay? You sound like hell."

"I just woke up but thanks for saying so. Once I get the energy to stand up and start my day, I'll be fine."

Megan laughed. "I'm sorry, I didn't mean it to come out like that."

"Yeah, yeah."

"So listen, do you think you'd be okay taking Jaiden Michael for the night? I know I only asked for a few hours, but Dana called and said plans had changed. We're going into the city tonight and we're supposed to get a room at some fancy hotel. The girls are insisting."

"Absolutely," Kathy said, knowing this would help her through her days off. A sound that came from the spare bedroom drew her attention.

"Thank you, I owe you big time."

Another sound came again, like someone was moving around in there, opening and closing the drawers or doors.

"Sam?" She grabbed the white silk robe that had been thrown over the chair in the corner of her room. Shaking it to remove the heavy wrinkles, she put it on, tied the belt snug around her waist and left her bedroom.

"Who is Sam?"

"What?" Kathy said.

"Are you okay? You're acting weird."

"Yeah, I'm fine."

"You sound really nasally. You should take something."

"I'm fine."

"You don't sound fine. Should I cancel?"

"No. I want him to come. I think I need him to come."

She listened to the noise growing louder as she slowed her approach.

"You there?"

"Yeah. I had this crazy dream last night."

"About what?"

"Rocco driving the limo and it was my wedding day, but the weird thing was the limo was smashed and I wasn't married to him."

"That's crazy. Who were you getting married to?"

She stopped and so did the sounds. "I don't know. That's the weirdest part. I don't know who he is."

"Well, it was just a dream. Are you okay?"

"Yeah, I'm good. Are you still bringing him over around six?"

"Yes."

"That's perfect. I'm going to go now."

"Are you sure you're okay?"

"Yeah, I'm fine. I want to take my meds and run a hot shower. I'll see you when you get here," she said, and hung up the phone.

Tiptoeing down the hallway, she listened at the door. The sound of what she thought was fabric ripping and grunts influenced her to knock on the door. It swung open enough for her to see inside. Sam sat at the head of the bed. His feet were on the floor and he was removing the bandages she wrapped his wounds with.

"You should be lying down and resting."

Kathy pushed the door open and entered the room. She stared at him and made no effort to hide her confusion. Eying the blood-dried wrappings that were on the night table, her focus shifted to Sam's tattered pants on the floor next to the bed. Looking back at him, the cuts and bruises that riddled his body were now gone, appearing to have healed with no sign of their ever having been there a few hours before.

"I'm feeling much better today," he said. "You wouldn't happen to have any spare clothes for me to wear, would you?"

Kathy shook her head no, unable to speak the word or explain what she was seeing. Sam stood and wrapped the blanket around his waist. He grabbed his pants and approached Kathy and stopped.

"Excuse me," he said, and Kathy hesitated.

"Oh," she said, realizing he needed to pass. She moved out of his way and he exited the bedroom and went into the bathroom.

A few moments later he came out dressed in the bloodstained tattered rags she found him in the night before. He returned the blanket to the bed and stood before her and looked into her eyes. He took her hand into his own, and said, "I want to thank you for helping me last night. I assure you that I am undeserving of such compassion but it is heartfelt and appreciated. I'm sure your kind heart hasn't gone unnoticed. If only I knew what I was doing when I committed those horrible acts, believe me, I wouldn't have ever done them. I've learned and have changed since then. Please believe me."

"I do," she said without reason, and remembered her lack of control around him when he slept and the way she acted towards him in her dream. She was putty in his hands and she couldn't resist it.

Sam kissed the back of her hand and turned and started to walk off. The confusion inside Kathy was unsettling. There were so many things surrounding this man that she couldn't explain. He was troubled by his life's decisions and was plagued by someone's need for revenge.

"Where are you going?" she said.

"I must leave you."

"What about the people that are after you?"

"I think it best if I don't provide any details of what brought us together. I need to take my leave now before the mess I've created begins to affect you."

The feeling of panic made her eager. She couldn't just let him leave, not like this. There was a bad feeling all around her that she couldn't ignore. Sam turned the knob on the front door and in a moment of desperation she caught a glimpse of Sam from her dream at the forest's edge. She suddenly remembered the beautiful man with the glowing red eyes. *He called Sam by a name. What was it?*

"Who is Sardurvial and why am I better off with no answers?" she said.

Sam paused, bowed his head and then slowly looked over his shoulder at her.

"This is getting dangerous much faster than I expected. They've gotten to you in one night, and for both your sake and my own, I need to leave."

"How can I convince you to stay?"

Sam shook his head. "You don't understand. You can't."

Kathy felt obligated. "Not even for another few hours? Just allow me to help you get things together. I'll get you some clothes, you can bathe while I'm gone, then I'll feed you. If you allow me to do this, then I'll have peace of mind and you can leave right after."

Kathy knew the timing of her plan was absolutely perfect. Sam would be showered, clothed, fed, and out the door before Megan arrived with Jaiden Michael. And maybe when this was all over her compassion would have helped change the fate of someone in need.

Sam sighed heavily. "I couldn't. If anything were to happen to you, I would never be able to forgive myself. I've witnessed one person suffer in ways you could never imagine and that's enough to haunt me forever. Trust me when I tell you it is best I go."

"You can't expect people not to notice you with the clothes you have on," Kathy said. "You'll stand out like a sore thumb. You need my help."

Sam paused, knowing what she said was right. He couldn't possibly provide for himself once he set off on his own, and he wasn't about to start stealing and robbing. Sin was what Belial desired and he no longer wished to please him. It was obvious Kathy gave him his best chance at being able to flourish and blend into the populace. That way he would be able to lose his enemies until he could figure out what to do next. Maybe this woman was an offering from the Heavens. Divine intervention through means he wasn't meant to understand.

He above any knew anything was possible.

"If I stay for a few hours," Sam said, "Then I have to be insistent we don't discuss my past. And if I'm ever able to repay the kind gesture of helping you then you'll allow me to do so with thoughtful regard. Do we have a deal?"

Kathy smiled. "We have a deal."

Saturday, October 15th, 11:40 am

"I'm leaving now," Kathy said. "I should be back within an hour or so."

Sam emerged from the spare bedroom. "I would go with you—"

"But it's too risky, I know," she said, her voice sounded strange because of the cold. "This will give you a chance to clean yourself up and give me a chance to get some fresh air."

She retreated into the foyer and Sam followed. "Hey, Kathy?"

Kathy paused at the door. "Yes, Sam?"

"Thank you. I don't know how to tell you how much I appreciate your kindness, it's something I'm not used to nor something I deserve."

"I think differently," she said, and exited the apartment. Sam stood motionless for a moment while he listened to the sound of her footsteps fading away as she descended the worn wooden steps.

Sam entered the bathroom, started the shower, and peeled off the soiled clothes. He stood before the mirror and examined his flesh, touching where the most severe wounds stained his skin before he slept. He cringed. The exterior abrasions and bruises had all healed, but beneath the skin he still felt tender. He knew the broken bones hadn't fully healed yet and would probably need one more night.

He pulled open the mirror and quickly located the pills Kathy gave him the night before. Taking a handful out of the bottle, he closed the medicine cabinet and in the reflection standing behind him was a pale skinned girl with bright red hair and deep purple bruises covering her neck. She struggled to breathe and reached for Sam. He gasped and quickly turned around.

But he was alone.

The sudden movement aggravated the bruising on his side and it thundered with pain. He ignored it as best he could because his concern was on the little girl he saw in the mirror. He knew it was Redhead. Her pain, her suffering, her death, was his fault and there was nothing he could do to change that now.

"I was a bastard and I'm sorry," he said into the room and began to sob.

Stepping into the shower, he twirled underneath the warm flow of water and grabbed the soap from the soap dish. He began to wash himself and was gentle at first, but soon began vigorously scrubbing his body.

CHAPTER 7

THE BIRTH OF SIN
10,000 BC

Belial entered a vast, luxurious sleeping chamber decorated with elaborate furniture padded with plush hides from animals long ago extinct. A bed in the center of the room was encased with netting made from strands of gold, but Belial looked away unimpressed.

A simple reading chair and chest was in the corner of the room, and it was the contents of that chest he wanted to explore. He believed within its dark maw was the greatest prize ever created. According to the information he had gathered, this prize was so invaluable, the power and information it held could have possibly been more powerful than the entity that created it.

What would it look like?

His flesh goosed.

Could its power be controlled?

His willingness to risk everything to test that theory made him anxious.

How about altered?

His heart pounded. That was the ultimate question. That was what he hoped.

For the moment, the answers to all of the questions that raced through his mind would have to wait. He had to be sure everything was exactly the way it should be before he proceeded with his plan that took hundreds of years to flesh out.

Quietly retreating to the rear of the room where he opened swinging doors that gave way to a spacious balcony. Stepping onto the terrace, Belial looked out on the vast land where serenity had forever reigned undisturbed. But he knew about a secret hidden so deep, once it was brought to the surface it would fracture everything and everyone he knew. He dreamed it.

He closed his eyes, licked the cool air and inhaled deeply. Nothing was going to stop him. This day the untainted peace would be shattered forever and sides would be drawn. Some friends would turn on one another, creating a rift and two sources of rule. The two sides would clash throughout eternity.

"Mine will be better," Belial said. "Stronger."

Belial opened his eyes and exhaled heavily. He looked about the land below him and saw inactivity all around. The towering luxury apartments that housed Heaven's residents were all quiet. The streets, parks and lakes were completely abandoned. The sky was also quiet; not a soul hovered or soared about.

Everything was perfect, just like he'd planned it to be. God called the residents out for a celebration and it had something to do with the people he meddled with. Belial cared nothing for them and used the opportunity to his advantage. When no one was looking, he slipped out.

"Because I am smarter."

His flesh goosed with the statement. Everything was perfect and he was ready. This was a sign, he believed, because everything was playing out exactly as he planned; he was destined for something greater than any glory heaven could offer him. And at this moment he could only imagine what it was going to be like.

He turned and peered back into the sleeping chambers he entered uninvited. It was empty for the moment and probably for not much longer than that if anyone realized he was gone. Someone would be able to piece together his claims and reveal his plans. So he reentered the room and ran his hand over the soft skins that covered the reading chair and moved to the bed and sat. It was all so distracting. The bed sank slightly and conformed to his body perfectly. Comfortable, he lay prone, crossing his legs and interlacing his fingers behind his head. The elaborate design on the ceiling deserved his admiration. "This is all so very nice, Lord, but I will have better one day. I beg you to underestimate me."

Belial forced himself to stand and settled beside the chest. Hesitating in a moment of indecision, he fought the reluctance away and confidently slid the latch back. Grasping the handle in preparation of lifting the heavy marble top, he paused to consider everything. What he was about to do couldn't be undone once he lifted the lid. His life and the life of others would be changed forevermore, but it was his destiny to usher in change. Nodding in agreement with his inner voice, he lifted the lid.

The Heavens wept because they would never be the same.

Peering inside the chest, Belial was awestruck by what he unveiled: a thick book with golden pages. It had a cover carved from a precious gem unseen by his eyes and it glimmered in the flooding light that beamed in from the unobstructed balcony. Batting his eyes in an attempt to thwart the elegant glare, he couldn't help but look.

Magical.

He hesitated because he was afraid to smudge the beauty. Reaching his shaking hand out and caressing the smooth cool cover, a chill raced through his body and the power of his discovery coursed through his fingertips and penetrated his blackened soul. He was alive and free of the oppression at last!

He opened the cover and scanned the hieroglyphic writing within. Every symbol had great meaning and he knew them all. This discovery was better than expected. To imagine its power could be controlled and now it was his!

Closing the book, he reached his other hand inside the box. Wrapping both hands around the giant book and lifting it from its home, its weight was tremendous but Belial's strength was greater.

In the moments between kneeling and fully standing upright, he couldn't help but think how he would prove everything he had said. With the book in his possession, vast knowledge was his and it would guide him as he ruled.

Now he was whole.

He could begin his reign without fear or regret.

With pride and a touch of arrogance, he tittered. The residents of Heaven that secretly followed him would no longer have to do it from the shadows. They could joyously announce their faith in him and he would be their leader; the creator and destroyer as he saw fit.

Belial lifted a foot and defiantly kicked down the cover of the chest; it slammed shut and the fine marble chipped. Belial laughed at what was now imperfect.

He exited the room and stood on the balcony, holding the book tightly against his chest, protecting the secrets contained within its pages, keeping it to himself. Climbing on the railing and balancing himself, the serenity abroad sickened him.

Leaping outwards, his stately wings snapped open and caught the air. Onwards he glided, the currents he rode took him well away from his world and into another. Choosing a secreted location, he buried the book deep in the dirt. Stomping the freshly packed ground flat, the earth trembled.

"Now it's time for the oppression of my people to end."

CHAPTER 8

AN ACT OF KINDNESS

Saturday, October 15th, 3:45 pm

Kathy fought her way up the narrow flight of stairs and the two bulky bags she carried rubbed the walls and slowed her progress. Reaching the locked door to her apartment, she placed one bag down and shuffled through her pocketbook in search of her house keys. She sneezed, hooting loudly, and her body trembled violently. Pausing for the pain that didn't come, she worked the door lock open and moved the bag on the floor inside the apartment with her foot while she worked the key out of the lock with her free hand. Pushing the door closed with her hip, she placed the second bag next to the other and Sam seemed to appear out of nowhere.

"I didn't hear you coming up the stairs or I would have helped you," Sam said.

"That's okay," Kathy said. "I could use the exercise." She turned her attention to the bags and began to pull the garments out one at a time. "I bought you two pairs of pants, some sneakers, and a couple of shirts. I took a guess at your sizes, so I need you to try everything on. And if you don't mind, when you try the clothes on I would like you to come out of the bathroom so I can see how everything fits."

Sam smiled and took the clothes. "That's the least I can do for you," he said, and headed to the bathroom.

Kathy sneezed and Sam looked at her. "God bless you," he said, and turned and stepped into the bathroom. "Someone like you should be in His favor."

"Thank you," Kathy said and tried to smile but winced instead. The pain in her lower back was excruciation.

Sam entered the room and watched Kathy place a bowl of pasta in the microwave and set the table for two, pour two drinks of soda, and retrieve the heated dish of pasta out of the microwave. Gliding about, she served both plates, covered and placed the tray of pasta in the center of the table and admired her work.

"Well," Sam said, stepping into Kathy's view. "How does it look?"

Kathy looked at Sam and inspected him from head to toe. "Now you can go out and not have to worry about everyone staring at you."

"I feel much better," he said, and brushed his hand over the clothes, admiring the perfect fit. "Thank you for doing this."

"You're welcome," she said with a smile. "Now let's eat." She sat at the table.

Sam sat too, and looked at his plate with delight. He savored the dish with his eyes, tasted it with a long sniff, but refrained from taking his fork because he didn't want to give the impression as being bad mannered. His stomach growled painfully, but he was determined to ignore the ache until Kathy extended a formal invitation for him to eat.

"Please, dig in while it's hot," she said, the congestion in her sinuses noticeable to Sam. The sound of her voice was muted and her eyes were watery.

He watched her use her fork to delicately gather the pasta, blow on it, and take a tiny bite.

"You're a good person Kathy," he said, and she smiled. But there was so much more to the meaning behind that than just words. The girl he knew as Redhead was just like her.

The telephone on the wall beside the refrigerator rang. Kathy rolled her eyes and wiped her mouth.

"It never fails. Excuse me," she said, and picked up the telephone. "Hello?" she said, and walked into the hallway where she wouldn't disturb Sam.

"Hi, Kathy, this is Claire. I hate to do this, but do you think you'll be able to come in tonight around 8:00? Before you answer, I'm begging you not to say no because I really need you and it'll only be for a few hours. You know I wouldn't bother you on your days off, especially knowing you don't feel well, but I don't have anyone else to turn to."

Kathy felt cornered by Claire's desperate plea and almost blurted her agreement. She considered Claire to be more than an acquaintance from work. She was a good friend who had been there when Rocco died. She was there every step of the way through her rehabilitation and that made her feel indebted.

But no matter her dedication or need to please her friend, it was impossible for her to be there. Her cold was knocking her around and she promised to watch her nephew.

"I'm sorry, Claire, I really am. Jaiden Michael is coming over later on and my cold seems to be getting worse. Megan is finally going out with her girlfriends, and like it or not, I have him for the night. You know it kills me to have to tell you no, but I'm sure you understand."

Claire was silent for a moment and it just killed her knowing that was really just disappointment in disguise. She could hear the non-stop activity of the hospital in the background and it sounded like a madhouse.

"I'm sorry Claire, I really am."

Claire breathed into the phone. "Oh no, I'm getting my brains beat in. Are you sure there's no possible way? You know I wouldn't put you in this position if I didn't exhaust all of my other resources. I have no one else. While you are here, you could get one of the doctors to write you a prescription. It'll be to 11:00 tonight, no later, I promise."

Kathy closed her eyes and massaged her temples; she could feel the clog in her head causing a sinus headache. She took a few moments to mull over her options and eventually concluded there weren't any. She sighed heavily, leaned against the wall, and said, "I would help you if I could, Claire, you know that. But my hands are tied. I already promised Megan I would watch Jaiden Michael and I can't break that promise. This night is too important to my sister and I couldn't possibly cancel on her. It really kills me to have to tell you no. I'm sorry."

"Excuse me. Kathy!" Sam said, from the table. He got up and walked to her.

"Hold on a second Claire." She covered the mouthpiece.

"I know this offer may sound a bit strange to you," he said, "but I could watch Jaiden for a few hours while you are gone. I don't mind, and besides, this will allow you to help your friend out, get some medicine for that cold I hear, and allow me to repay you for your kindness."

Kathy searched for a reason and way to politely decline. To allow a total stranger to watch a child not his own or even family was ludicrous. But, as she looked into Sam's eyes, the thought of how senseless it really was never registered. His eyes were saying something that couldn't be ignored.

Sam shared a comforting smile. "I will care for him, Kathy. You know deep down inside I would never let harm come to the boy."

Kathy knew that was the message she was getting from his eyes and she believed every word of it. Without contemplation, she uncovered the phone. "Claire? Yeah, I'll be able to come in for a few hours to help you out. Hang tight, I'll see you around 8:00."

"You're not kidding with me, are you?"

"No, I'm coming to help you out."

"How did you—"

"It doesn't matter. I'll see you in a little while."

Kathy hung up the telephone, and absorbed by Sam's gaze that stayed with her long after he turned away, she watched him return to the table.

CHAPTER 9

THE PEOPLE

Saturday, October 15th, 6:28 pm

Standing in the bathroom, Kathy blew her reddened nose and examined her watering eyes in the mirror.

"This is just great," she said, and moved closer to the mirror. Her eyes were bloodshot and purple bags hung beneath them. Three loud knocks coming from the front door prompted her to look at the clock.

6:29

Her sister had arrived with Jaiden Michael. She hurried to the door and passed Sam along the way. He sat on the couch and watched television with the remote in hand. He flipped from channel to channel, staring at the television. A look of disbelief twisted his expression into something unpleasant.

"You okay?" Kathy said.

"They talk about one tragedy after another," he said. "It seems like there is nothing to talk about other than violence and suffering."

"That's why I don't watch the news," Kathy said. Sliding the deadbolt back and removing the door chain, she opened the door and smiled brightly at her nephew and sister. "Hi guys," she said, enthused, and smothered her young nephew with a tight hug.

Jaiden's arms were pinned to his side and he didn't resist her.

"Come on in," Kathy said sniffling, and she helped Jaiden get out of his coat. "Oh, look at you," she said, and hugged him again. "You're wearing the sweater I got you."

"I told you she would like it," Megan said. She was wearing an oversized red wool turtleneck sweater that hung off her squared shoulders. Matching gloves and a clingy pair of black leggings encouraged her to give her sister the once over. "You look good," she said.

Megan joined in and helped tend to Jaiden. "Thank you Faye, that's nice of you to say. So what about you, how are you feeling?"

"I'm doing fine."

"Are you sure? I think your cold sounds worse than it did this morning. Maybe I should cancel tonight so you can rest."

"Don't be silly. I have the sniffles, not the Ebola virus."

Megan scrutinized her sister. "Are you sure you're up to this?"

"He's like my bottle of medicine," Kathy said, and drew Jaiden in with another hug. "Don't start looking for excuses. You're going tonight and that's that."

Megan tilted her head and was quiet in her consideration. "You sure?"

"As one could be."

Megan smiled appreciatively. "If there are any problems with him, call these numbers I wrote out for you." Megan handed her sister a sheet of paper with emergency numbers scribbled on it. She squatted before her son, placed her hands on both of his shoulders, looked directly into his eyes, and said, "Now remember what I told you. Listen to your aunt and don't give her a hard time. She's not feeling well tonight so don't ask her to follow you all over. You understand?"

Jaiden nodded.

Kathy rolled her eyes.

Kathy looked into the television room and motioned for Sam to come over. She turned back to her sister. "Megan, I want you to meet a friend of mine from the hospital. His name is Sam."

Sam came into the room and shook Megan's hand. "It is very nice to meet you," he said, smiling. He turned his attention to Jaiden and offered him his hand. "And it is very nice to meet you too, young man. You must be Jaiden."

Jaiden lazily responded to Sam with a weak uninterested handshake and headed for the closet in the living room. He began removing some toys packed inside a laundry basket.

Sam watched Jaiden with noticeable curiosity.

"And make sure you clean up after yourself," Megan shouted, and then smiled. "Well, I should get going. Thank you for watching him tonight. It was really nice to meet you, Sam."

"And it was nice meeting you, too," he said, and shook Megan's hand again. He turned and left for the television room.

Kathy walked her sister to the door. "Have a good time tonight."

Megan smiled. "I'll try, and you do the same." She winked and strolled into the hallway. "But wait until Jaiden goes to bed."

"Jerk," Kathy said smiling, and closed the door. She locked the bolt and slid the chain back on. She rarely ever used the deadbolt let alone the useless chain. It was flimsy and she knew it wouldn't provide her with very much protection if any at all. She could remember seeing an actor playing the part of an intruder on the news. He approached a door with a chain lock and just laid a heavy shoulder into it, ripping the chain from the frame. But any little obstacle might help, she figured, consciously aware that Sam's concerns were quickly becoming her own.

She went into the living room where Sam was sitting on the floor with Jaiden. The two were running Matchbox cars through the rug, playing imaginatively. She watched them in silence and was pleased how quickly Jaiden took to Sam. He seemed caring, patient and was good with children. What else could a woman want? She was comforted knowing the two would be fine together once she left for work.

Kathy exited the room and retreated to her bedroom to change into her work uniform. She kicked off her black boots, hopped around as she peeled off her jean pants, and struggled to pull the tight neck of her shirt over her head without messing her hair.

And as she dressed into her work clothes, she could hear the laughter of both Sam and Jaiden through her closed door. She smiled in satisfaction. All of her fears and worries diminished completely that moment.

She slipped on her winter jacket and walked into the hallway by the front door.

"Sam?" she said.

She heard him stand, and the subsequent low thuds of his approaching footsteps. He rounded the corner and stopped before her. His eyebrows rose in an inquisitive gesture.

"I'm going to run out to the store really fast to get Jaiden some snacks. Do you want me to bring you anything back?"

"No, thank you."

"Okay," she said. "I'm going to have a quick word with him before I go."

Sam watched Jaiden play with toy cars. The innocence of a child captivated him and he couldn't hold back a smile knowing that hadn't completely left the world. Overwhelming mixes of emotions consumed him and he didn't attempt to resist them. Each element of his feelings was completely painful yet didactic. And strangely enough, they were simple to define. The joy he felt proved he was truly happy for the first time since the turn of events that brought him to that dark stairwell one night ago. The sadness he felt was for having ever allowed himself to be misguided and swayed by the others. He could only speculate how one could follow another so blindly then suddenly have the ability to see things so clearly. He remembered on his day of reckoning how God told him that those he followed were no good and the people of the world were precious. The lies he saw in that statement were sickening to him and the insulting statement echoed around his head and bothered him for years.

One witnessing God's odd behavior and the way Belial analyzed it, you would never believe the people were precious. After all, it was the people that were responsible for taking His attention away from them. They were responsible for their misfortune because they infringed on the splendor of Heaven and its Angels.

Now he realized it was his turn to play the fool. How could he have ever believed it was the people that were responsible? And to think that those he once believed loved him were after him, looking to make him an example . . .

The thought enraged him. He willingly ruined his eternal life, turned his back on God for them and this was how they treated him? It was all a big joke to him but he wasn't laughing.

How could he ever believe they were his friends to begin with?

Sardurvial snickered. *Friends.*

Throughout time he'd seen the signs, the warnings he should've paid attention to. There were so many that had been made an example of. There was Jeremiah, Christian and Jacob. Some were friends and others weren't. It really didn't matter to him at the time either. There was never any loyalty to any that would dissent. He didn't, just couldn't understand at the time why someone would suddenly undergo such a change and be willing to submit their life for something they stood so strongly against at one time. What was it they could see that the others couldn't? He couldn't understand it.

But he understood now because he was able to see what brought forth the change with his own eyes. It was a terrible experience he wouldn't soon forget.

Maybe what he said to the group yesterday was enlightening enough to move some of the other, more intelligent members of the community to investigate his findings. Maybe they would dig deep enough to find what he'd said to be the truth and they too would be brave enough to take a stand like he had. Sam could only pray such an occurrence would transpire. It would help free the people from the bondage and make the pain he had to endure well worth it.

The front door slammed and rattled the windows in their frames. The sound quickly pulled Sam from his thought and sent him to his feet. A new thought emerged: *I didn't lock the door when I walked Kathy out.*

"Hello Kathy, is that you?"

He waited and listened but didn't get a response.

His adrenaline soared. Swiftly advancing towards the door, Sam entered the hallway, seeing the door was already closed and locked, and the surrounding area was unoccupied. He moved onwards, devising a plan of attack in his mind. Once he located the mischievous fiends, he was going to draw them away from the boy. He realized they might've come for him to make him the example. He would fight whomever Belial sent for him, and do so until the death. His heart thundered and his palms began to sweat. The fear that could keep him from making a foolish mistake remained distant. He knew above anything else he must protect the boy.

He reached the ending of the hallway, and heard faint sounds that were purposely kept quiet that were coming from within the kitchen. There was no doubt his newly formed enemies were in there, preparing to carry out their original plan to get him. He clenched his fists, felt a surge of death defying willpower coursing through his veins as he leapt around the corner and prepared to deliver a precise killing blow.

Kathy turned around and screeched in fear. Sam pulled his punch, missing Kathy by mere inches.

A yogurt fell from Kathy's hands and hit the floor with a splat. The fruit syrup splattered out ten feet in all directions.

The refrigerator door tapped closed.

Kathy was holding her heart and her eyes were clamped tightly shut.

Sam was panting with his hands on his knees, his rage melding into relief.

"I'm sorry Kathy, I thought you were one of them. Why didn't you answer me when I called out to you?"

Kathy stared blankly at Sam then her focal point moved over his shoulder. She forced a laugh and Sam turned to see Jaiden standing in the threshold of the kitchen and hallway, his expression uneasy.

"I didn't hear you come up on me," she said with a laugh.

Sam smiled, following Kathy's mask. "I think your scream scared me worse."

They laughed and Kathy grabbed a DVD she'd placed on the counter earlier in the day and handed it to Jaiden. "Here, you're going to like this," she said, and started cleaning the yogurt off of the floor. Jaiden looked at the old DVD and case.

Sam lent her a hand. "Are you okay," he whispered. "I'm sorry I didn't mean to startle you."

Kathy nodded. "I'm okay."

"What're the Goonies?" Jaiden said, and continued to inspect the DVD case.

"It's a great movie I watched when I was a kid," Kathy said. "I dug it out of the archives so you could watch it. You'll love it, I know I did."

"Can Sam watch it with me?"

"That's up to Sam. Why don't you ask him?"

Sam didn't wait for Jaiden to ask. "Of course I'll watch it with you. Go turn on the television and start the movie, I'll be there in a minute."

Jaiden hurried into the living room. Sam looked at Kathy. "Are you still planning on leaving for work soon?"

"Yeah, I have to go in in about twenty minutes." She smiled. "I really don't think I need medicine anymore. Whatever was clogging my head was scared right out of me."

"Stop. I feel bad."

"I'm only kidding. That's my way of letting you know I'm okay."

Sam nodded and worked to get the mess up with a paper towel.

"Why don't you go and sit with Jaiden? I'll finish this. Once I'm done, I'm going to come in and tell him I have to go to work. I'm sure he'll be thrilled you're going to be looking after him. It's unlike him, but he's taking a real liking to you really fast."

Sam smiled but quickly repressed the satisfied feeling. It was a pleasure to be liked without having done something wicked to earn it. He stared into Kathy's eyes, remaining silent for a moment to place emphasis on his forthcoming statement. "Be careful tonight, Kathy, please. I mean it."

Kathy nodded without taking the pleading tone too seriously.

"They could have done something to lure you out of the house and it worries me."

"I'll be mindful, but I'll be fine."

Sam went to the television room and sat next to Jaiden on the couch. The previews for other movies started rolling.

A few minutes into the movie, Kathy came into the room and sat beside Jaiden and watched the movie with them for a little while. "I have to go to work for a few hours," she said. "Sam is going to watch you. Is this okay?"

Jaiden shook his head in acknowledgement. His focus remained on the television screen.

"If there are any problems," Kathy said, "or if you just need to talk to me, you can have Sam call me at work." She looked at Sam. "I wrote my work number on the pad next to the phone. I'll be home in a few hours."

Kathy kissed Jaiden, and mouthed the words, "Have fun" to Sam. Sam smiled and waved her away. Moments later, the front door closed and Sam went to lock it: knob, dead bolt and chain. He returned to Jaiden on the couch, and watched Chunk on the television shaking his belly in an attempt to get inside the house with the other Goonies.

Jaiden and Sam shared a laugh.

CHAPTER 10

MUTINY
10,000 BC

Belial approached a blissful insensible mass that was gathered around the Great Fountain on the outskirts of the mainland. The meeting was unmindfully unfolding to the blissful citizens of Heaven who went about their business in the city beyond them.

Some occupied the benches that surrounded the spring, and others sat on its frame, dipping their feet into the cool water, kicking and frolicking about without concern. Belial announced his nearness, being cheerful and confident in his declaration.

"Thank you for coming so quickly, friends!" Belial said. He wiped sweat from his brow and he breathed heavily. "I have great news to share with you today!"

All sitting around greeted his coming with delight and extreme favoritism; all stood and rushed to shake his hand and kiss his cheek. He was the answer to their prayers. Belial outwardly expressed his delight over the compassionate treatment and once the crowd settled, he took his place before them. They gave him their complete attention and Belial sensed the anticipation so he purposely took his time in moving to the fountain. He dunked his head to cool his beaded brow. Pulling his head from the water and throwing it back, Belial squeezed the excess water from his hair and groaned in delight. Continuing to move deliberately slow, he took his place in the center of his admirers.

"I want to forewarn everyone right now," Belial said, and a sense of tension came over the crowd. "That I'm ready to do as I said I would so long ago, and do so on this very day. I contemplated why I . . . Why we should put this off any longer. I'm going to approach the Throne of God and tell him how I feel about His love for mankind over us. The pain I felt in my heart so long ago is still ripe, and it guides me even to this day. If you all still wish to stand by my side, do so now when I confront Him. If you choose to stand by my side, I want you to do so without fear because I shall speak on your behalf, and I will do so without worry of retribution. I do this because I know we're right! But if your allegiance lies elsewhere, then I suggest you stay as far away from the lounge as you can. This day, the Heavens will quaver because of us!"

Belial began to pace, the thoughts stirring deep within his mind and heart silencing him, the worry of the crowd still thick and tense. Pausing in movement, he focused on a particular thought. "If you choose to stand by my side, I can promise you great things to come. For you see, I have gained control over something most powerful, something you may have forgotten about in the time that has passed since its mention. I've entered God's sleeping chamber and breached the chest last night. Inside the chest I found something I will have to put under great scrutiny and see how it will benefit us. But stand tall because what I could tell from just a glance, this item will benefit us all and give us the power we need to stand against Him!

Everyone around muttered in amazement and openly discussed Belial's unbelievable claim of thievery and the possession of great power in a wave of inaudible jabber. Belial watched them, knowing his claim guaranteed their support in the events to come.

"Those who support me and wish to stand by my side while I confront God, follow me now, and remember to do so proudly and without fear. As we make our way through the heart of the city, I want you to tell the others the same as I told you here. Ask them to choose their side. If they choose to follow us, tell them we'll be settling our difference in the lounge. We're going there because that is where God is and where I shall force our confrontation. Be prepared to be judged and to fight for what you believe in. From this day forward for our journey will not be easy but we will be free at last. Now let us go!"

Belial marched towards the city inside Heaven with a steadfast purpose. Everyone around began to cheer him while they followed close behind.

CHAPTER 11

INTRUDERS

Saturday, October 15th, 10:18 pm

Kathy completed her rounds over fifteen minutes ago and now sat at the nurse's station.

"I have to pee the Nile and afterwards I'm going to step outside for a quick smoke," Claire said.

"I think that's a good idea. I don't like it when you start getting grumpy," Kathy said.

"Well, you know how us smokers need to get our fix."

"No, I don't get it, but okay, whatever. We were so busy tonight I thought you forgot about having a cigarette."

Claire smiled. "Honey, I don't ever forget about my smokes."

"Well, go while you can," Kathy said.

Claire hurried away and Kathy blew her reddened nose and her ears popped.

"Ouch," she said, and opened her mouth wide. She busied herself by filing papers and neatening the cluttered desktop. With her focus firmly on the task at hand, she didn't hear or detect a young woman step off of the elevator and approach the nurse's station.

Busy minutes passed by before Kathy noticed something out of the corner of her eye. She looked and smiled at the woman that was hidden behind a bouquet of flowers she held.

"You walk so softly," Kathy said. "I didn't even hear you approach. It's been a busy night. I'm really sorry, but visiting hours are over for the night. The security guard shouldn't have let you up here."

The woman moved the flowers aside and smiled at Kathy. "That's okay," the woman said. "They didn't know I was coming up."

Kathy found the smile warm and comforting and remembered seeing this woman before.

Maybe she was the daughter of a patient that had come to thank her with flowers? It happened often, and she found that was one of the greatest rewards of the job. There were so many people who came in and out that she hardly got to know anyone personally.

"Can I help you with anything else?" Kathy said while she continued to try and place the face.

"No," the woman said, shaking her head gently. "But I've come to help you."

Kathy continued to study her.

"You need to trust my words and call home, Lady Kathy. Check on Jaiden Michael if only for the purpose of waking Sam."

Kathy stared at the woman, speechless. She quivered and suddenly made the connection. The woman that stood before her was the woman she encountered the night she was leaving. The strange occurrences of that night had started with this woman and continued with doctor Williams and ended with the discovery of Sam in the stairwell at her apartment.

Porcelain Face.

Kathy walked out from behind the desk while appraising the woman. She was beautiful beyond words, outwardly unafraid of Kathy's approach, and gentle and strong all at once.

"Lady Kathy," she said, and handed Kathy the flowers. "You must always remember that you're loved and those flowers are a symbol of that love. I need you to remain strong in these trying times."

"Who are you?"

"I'm a friend that can be trusted. Those who are looking to exact their revenge on Sam are dangerously close to him now. He needs to be roused so he can rightfully defend himself and the boy. Make the call, Lady Kathy, and do so without questioning what I say. It could mean the difference between life and death."

Kathy wanted to do as instructed but was stilled by her uncertainties. So many questions were spinning around her in a dizzying fray to understand.

"Who has come to harm Jaiden and Sam?" Kathy said.

"Legions that are bitter about their rejection," Porcelain Face said.

"How do you know these things?"

"Because I was there when they were rejected."

Ding.

Kathy turned to see Claire stepping out of the elevator.

"Thank you so much, Kathy," Claire said, and seemed oblivious to Porcelain Face. "I really needed that. You can call it a night if you want, your relief will be here any moment."

Claire brushed by Kathy, the strong odor of smoke filling her nostrils. It was a repulsive smell that often created a debate.

Claire settled behind the desk and Kathy moved her attention back to Porcelain Face.

No one was there.

Kathy looked down the long hospital corridor to her left and right in an attempt to spot the woman withdrawing, but she was nowhere to be found.

"You look pale to me," Claire said, and her words pulled Kathy from her confusion. "Is everything okay?"

Kathy continued to search the abandoned hallway and found no sign of the woman ever having been there. She held out her hands and saw the flowers she was holding were gone.

"I'm not really sure," Kathy said.

"You're making me nervous."

"Everything is fine. I just have to make a quick phone call. Is it okay if I use the back office?"

"Of course, but Kathy?"

Kathy gave pause.

"Are you sure you're okay? You're pale like you've seen a ghost," Claire said.

"I'm sure. I really need to go and make this call. I'll be right back."

And quickly she rushed to a phone in a quiet back office to call home in hopes of getting Sam.

Saturday, October 15, 10:28 pm

Sardurvial sat in the backseat of a two-door sedan dull in color and quiet in ride. Lenny drove the sedan down a two lane street, obeying every traffic sign exactly. The sedan approached a pedestrian crossing and a guard stepped out into the street. White gloves with a raised handheld stop sign and a reflective orange vest was easy to see. Lenny eased the car to a gentle stop. He was the first car in a long line and his timing couldn't have been better.

A group of high school kids shuffled across the street on the crossing guards command. Lenny observed the pack of children with interest, searching the small group for someone specific. He had his eye on this particular someone for a few weeks now and, as usual, with her head down and no one beside her, she walked across the street, passing just a few feet away from Lenny's bumper.

"Redhead," he panted.

Lenny sniffed the air and wanted to reach out and touch her. She would be vulnerable to his charm if he was given a fair chance to share it with her. He would give her roses, chocolate and maybe a stuffed animal to start. But he knew she would never give him a chance. So he wanted to use force because she would be submissive to his anger and strength. It would scare her. Either way she wanted to accept it was fine with him. Things would become real intense and passionate between them.

Stretched out in the back seat, Sardurvial watched Lenny, relaxed.

"I don't want you to wait anymore," Sardurvial said. "She's yours today if you want her."

Sardurvial gazed out the side window and looked at a car parked on the side of the road. A woman sat in her car searching a crowd of kids with intensity. He returned his attention to Lenny with a smirk.

"You see her?" Sardurvial said. "Now that's a smart woman. She knows full-well there are predators out there like you and she tries to keep her baby safe from them. Maybe I'll have you get her kid next to teach her a lesson. But for now, don't worry about what comes after Redhead. You need to remember the plan I've gone over with you and stick to it. It'll work and you can trust that."

Lenny inanely nodded and rubbed the sweat from his brow. His heart thundered in nervous anticipation. His groin stirred and he wanted her, needed her, and he would take her this day. Unlike so many

of the other days when he was so near, today everything seemed right.

The crossing guard moved out of the street and
motioned the traffic onwards.

"Don't let her see you," Sardurvial said, and
Lenny mindlessly obeyed the instruction and pulled
down the visor and looked out the passenger window
away from the girl.

"That a boy," Sardurvial said and smiled knowing
how proud Belial would be of him. He'd chosen the
perfect candidate and infiltrated his psyche.

"Now," Sardurvial said. "I want you to hurry to
the shortcut. Park your car away from the area. We're
going to get out, get into position, and wait for her to
come to us. Don't forget the tools. Do you understand
me?"

"Yes," Lenny said, the words he heard came from
what he thought was his conscious.

"Of course you do," Sardurvial said with a laugh.
There were things in the world that couldn't be com-
prehended by man because of the limitations of their
mind. People were worthless and were to be used like
cattle and he couldn't understand why God was so
infatuated with them.

Lenny drove the car three blocks away, a half block
away from the shortcut, and parked. He grabbed the
sack he'd prepared and placed on the passenger seat
floor earlier in the day and exited the car. Hurrying
into the woods, Sardurvial followed, watching Lenny's
every move, making sure everything he did was being
done exactly as he instructed.

Once well within the cover of the forest, Lenny removed a pair of rubber gloves from the sack and put
them on. He removed a ski mask and an old broken
gun, pulled the mask over his face and squatted in
a concealing cluster of bushes, waiting for the girl

to come. His knees clunked together nervously and the urge to relieve his full bladder was so intense it almost drove him from the brush.

"Stay there and keep quiet," Sardurvial said.

Lenny obeyed and Sardurvial remained in the narrow pathway, watching, waiting to give Lenny the signal of the girl's approach.

Five minutes went by before the unmistakable sound of leaves rustling underfoot stirred Sardurvial's attention into the overgrown distance. He concentrated his gaze on the vantage point of the path to verify the approaching person was the girl Lenny desired. The glow of her auburn hair and pale skin reflected the angled sunbeams peaking through the treetops like a blood-soaked piece of foil.

Redhead arrived and obliviously walked towards something terrible.

Sardurvial smiled with satisfaction knowing what was about to happen to her. He'd gone through this a thousand times before, but this time, something made it different for him. He'd spent a lot of time planning this one out and found that he had taken a certain liking to the girl. What was there not to like? She was quiet and respectful even to those who mistreated her. She was smart and had a wonderful imagination, one that might benefit the world if she was ever given the chance to develop and share those ideas. But she was a victim and had always been one, and tragically, this day would fair to be no different than any of the others for her. In fact, it was going to be just a bit worse.

Sardurvial turned to Lenny. "Here she comes so ready yourself."

Lenny crouched low, preparing to spring, and he dependently squeezed the handle of the gun and watched the dense path with widened eyes. He couldn't yet see her but could hear her approach and his heart began to thunder again. His groin began to swell; he could only imagine what their union was going to be like. What he imagined was pure, just like he knew Redhead was. And these thoughts were delightful to Sardurvial.

The pale-faced girl treaded the path seemingly deep in thought, oblivious to the threat around her. Sardurvial could hear her thoughts too. School projects and the dream of a boy, the most popular one in school captured her attention. What chance would she have of being able to get someone like him to notice someone like her? She deniably shook her head knowing there wasn't any. She quickly pushed the thought from her mind and shifted her backpack from one shoulder to the other; its weight was causing an unbearable ache.

Lenny watched her approach and pass, and Sardurvial grew eager. "Do it," he coached, rubbing his hands together with delight. Sardurvial knew he should leave; it was the rule, but this one was different for him. He needed to see it, and besides, what did it matter if he watched? Nothing would come of it and no one would ever know.

Lenny hopped up and ran to catch up to Redhead. The branches grabbed at his legs and snapped loudly, alerting Redhead to his advance. The sudden rush of fear pushed her off the path and she turned to see what caused it.

"No, no, no!" Lenny said. "Don't look at me. I have a gun!" He grabbed her by the shoulder and pushed the pistol into her side, wiggling it around so she could feel the hardness of the barrel.

Redhead tensed. Her will to survive sobered her instantly and she obeyed his command by keeping her eyes forward.

Sardurvial remained at a distance and pondered his discoveries on human nature throughout time. Consistently he'd seen there were two types of people: the barbarians from birth and the quiet non-confrontational victims of the world and its savage inhabitants. In this moment, he'd come to realize that no matter how you look at either breed, in the end, they were all the same. They were weak beasts trying to play a grand game of life in an arena they have no understanding of.

"To your knees!" Lenny demanded.

Redhead continued to obey his commands without thought of resisting and she dropped to her knees. Her spit was thick and the tears flowed silently from her eyes. So young; she wasn't ready to die. "Please, don't hurt me," she muttered and let out a whimper.

Lenny scowled. His emotional and physical stimulation quickly turned to anger. He squeezed the handle of the gun. "When did I say I was going to hurt you? Why would you think to say such a thing?"

Redhead silently prayed and Sardurvial walked before her. He could hear more than her thoughts now. He could feel her fear, too. It moved beyond her body and into her soul and began to seep into his. Unseen, he drew himself inseparably near, watching from a closeness he'd been forbidden to take. A stupid rule he once thought, but now he understood why. The pain and fear of the victim could be felt and not escaped. It leaked from the body, the fear did, and it polluted the air like an airborne toxin that was being breathed in.

Sardurvial's heart raced with uncertainty, and his mind was overwhelmed with the moment. Paralyzed, he knew he should leave while he still had the chance. But he couldn't because something was keeping him there, something that was unseen to the unseen. The first thought was it was a lesson from the Heavens for all the crime and violence he influenced throughout time. Then he realized this might be the day of his judgment and punishment coming in a form that was beyond his understanding.

"Put your hands behind your back and don't make another sound," Lenny said. His tone was sharp. "If you do, I swear, you'll regret it!"

"Please listen to him," Sardurvial said.

Redhead accommodated Lenny and continued to do so without resistance. Sardurvial sighed a breath of relief, believing the girl would survive this. Sardurvial learned a valuable lesson to obey the rules Belial strictly enforced.

Lenny fumbled with the duct tape, and unable to grasp it, he pulled the gloves from his hands and found the lost end. He tore off a piece and placed it over Redheads mouth. His anger was subsiding some and he tried to muster a gentler tone when he spoke. "I understand you're scared, but if you do what I say and just keep quiet, you'll make it out of this alright."

Lenny wrapped the tape around Redhead's wrists, securing her hands behind her back. He then took the ski mask off his head and went to place it backwards on Redhead's head. She shifted, trying to resist being placed in the darkness of the hood; she hated and feared the darkness and now Sardurvial suddenly found he hated and feared the darkness too. Panicked, Redhead grunted and imagined she was being smothered. Sardurvial gasped and jolted forward, wanting to intervene, knowing this was a bad idea to stay behind and watch, but he couldn't move. The darkness was closing in all around him. Redhead turned quickly and faced Lenny to beg for his mercy. Lenny froze, disbelieving what Redhead had done.

Sardurvial froze in his struggle. He trembled in fear of the pain he knew was going to come.

Lenny's shoulders went limp and he lowered his chin. Closing his eyes, he shook his head. "Why'd you have to go and do that?" he said.

Lenny looked back at Redhead; her eyes wide and blue, her skin tight and appearing so virgin. Her innocence vibrated as her young body trembled. He was going to have to kill her and Lenny knew Redhead understood that because it was all being conveyed through Sardurvial somehow. She had seen his face and that left him with no choice. Her unwillingness to cooperate cost her that and he was saddened by the great loss. She might have been a good friend.

Lenny quickly drew the broken pistol back and struck Redhead on top of her head with the handle. Her skin split and sprayed Lenny and the surrounding brush with blood. Feeling the sting of the attack, Sardurvial reared and dropped to his knees. He watched Redhead slump forward and hit the ground. Her breathing was shallow and Sardurvial's breath shortened as he gasped along with her. He wanted to scream at Lenny, to make him stop, but he wheezed and fell to his side. The top of his head throbbed with pain and his ears rang. Now lying beside Redhead and staring into her face, Sardurvial watched the blood pour from the torn flesh atop her head. The ringing in his ears grew louder and he stirred.

Confusion came and took over.

Sam jumped from the couch and heaved in hysteria. His balance was off and he found his eyes were having trouble finding focus. He looked at Jaiden stretched across the couch, breathing slowly, snoring lightly as he slept.

"Just a dream," Sardurvial whispered. But it wasn't just a dream. It was a horrific memory. One he couldn't escape.

The television screen was blue, the Goonies movie over. The phone rang again and Sam realized that was the sound that pulled him from his sleep and not the buzzing of Redheads pain.

He hurried to the phone. "Hello?"

"Sam? It's Kathy." Her voice was loud.

Sam pulled his ear away from the receiver. He stumbled and leaned against the wall, rubbed his eyes and searched for the clock. It read 10:40.

"Hi, Kathy," he breathed, and rubbed his achy head at the temples. "We must've fallen asleep not too long after you left. I don't think we made it half-way through the movie."

"Is everything alright there? How is Jaiden?"

Sam rubbed his eyes and shook his head to try and dislodge the confusion. He looked in on Jaiden and he was sound asleep. "Yeah, everything is fine. Why do you sound so worried? Did something happen?"

"No, nothing happened. It has been a busy night and I'd been meaning to check in. If you want you can leave Jaiden Michael on the couch or put him in the spare bed where you slept last night. I should be home within the hour. Was he good for you?"

"Like an angel," Sam said, and continued to look at Jaiden.

"Good. I'll see you in a little while."

"Okay," Sam said and hung up the telephone. He returned to the television room and placed one arm around Jaiden's upper back and the other behind his knees. He picked Jaiden up off the couch and walked him to the spare bedroom.

Jaiden, half awake, squinted in the bright hallway lights, and wrapped his arms around Sam's neck. He buried his head in his chest and let out a deep sigh.

Entering the spare bedroom where Sam spent his first night, he pulled the covers back and placed Jaiden in the bed. He pulled the covers over him and started to walk out of the room.

"Sam?" Jaiden said.

Sam stopped. With the hallway light to his back, his body cast a giant shadow on the floor, wall and ceiling, consuming Jaiden in complete darkness.

"Yes, Jaiden?" he said.

"I've gotta say prayer before I go to bed for the night."

Sam walked to the bedside and pulled the covers back. Jaiden slid out of bed and knelt beside it. He rested his elbows on the mattress and said, "If I die before I wake, I pray the Lord my soul to take. Please bring my father back home. Amen."

Jaiden hurried back into bed and Sam covered him again. He walked out of the room and partially closed the door, and there he paused to try and fight the tears that welled in his eyes.

"The people really are precious," he said. "Why couldn't I see this before?"

Sam shut the hallway light off and walked to the television room. He sat on the couch and pondered his dream, trying to fight off the vivid details that troubled him in awareness. He shuddered.

"That poor girl," he said. "What did I do?"

Bang.

Sam jumped to his feet and fear consumed him. There was no way Kathy could have made it home that fast.

The sound came from the opposite side of the apartment he occupied, the side he laid Jaiden in. He moved swiftly to check on the boy and heard the shower running in the bathroom as he passed it.

Pushing the spare bedroom door open, Sam could clearly see the boy had already fallen asleep.

Scrutinizing the closed bathroom door, he smelled a trap but saw there was no way to avoid it. He had to confront the others if they discovered his whereabouts and came for him inside the house. He'd placed the family in terrible danger and he had to defend them.

Sam dropped to his knees and peered beneath the door. He felt the hot air within the bathroom rushing past his face and couldn't see anything beyond the lingering haze within the room. He couldn't help but think how the design of the bathroom allowed his pursuers to set a perfect trap. Concealing corners and a thick haze was to his disadvantage.

He reached up and as quietly as possible, twisted the door handle. The latch slid back and clicked when it cleared. The sound was dull but resonated boomingly to Sam. He paused and waited for a reaction from those he knew were on the other side of that door.

Moments passed and nothing happened. He inched the door open and kept his focus sharp, searching the murky air to try and spot the slightest movement, the slightest color change within the swirling gray mist. His neck was uncomfortably bent and he was exhausted, but this was about survival and he had to stay focused.

Sam stood and pushed the door open fully. The hinges whined and goosed Sam's clammy skin. His body trembled and he backed away.

He watched the cool air from the hallway rush inside the bathroom and collide with the mist. Engaged in a mystical battle, Sam watched the two sides blend chivalrously without remnants.

Sam's nerves calmed some when, to his surprise, he found there was no one inside the immediate vicinity of the bathroom. Had the shower been turned on to warn him of their nearness, of their ability to strike at any time? He shuddered at the thought and should have fled the moment Kathy uttered his true name: Sardurvial. Belial had gone into Kathy's dream to introduce himself, and quite possibly, to reveal secrets of his eternal kindred.

Sam cautiously walked to the shower; the *pitter-patter* of water was loud but concealed by the drawn curtain. He moved to the side of the drape and flicked it open.

Frozen by instant terror, Sam looked down on a beautiful saddened young man who cradled the Redhead girl from his dream. They were both beneath the showering spray, rocking gently, trying to clean deep gashes that riddled her body. The water racing for the drain was bloody and the girl was in pain, ululation her only release. The young man tried to comfort the girl. "You're going to be okay," the young man said.

"No, it's not going to be okay. I can feel it," Redhead said. "Please, make the water hotter, I'm really cold."

"The water is so hot it's scolding your skin," the young man said.

"Oh no," she whimpered, and suddenly her cries were hushed.

Her attention moved to Sam. "He was one of the men that did this to me." She pointed at Sam, barely able to lift her arm. "I saw him standing around watching me die!"

The beautiful young man that held Redhead became angry at the accusation. He eased the bleeding girl down and stood, looking fuming mad while he appraised Sam.

"You did this?"

Sam was frozen by his terror.

The air snapped and Sam reared. Giant wings behind the beautiful man fluttered and carried him towards Sam. Sam turned to run but collapsed in his weakness and cowered on the floor.

"Sardurvial," Belial said, and Sardurvial trembled at the sound of his voice. "Stand and face me, traitor."

He stood, glimpsing the empty bathtub before he did. He swallowed hard. The cold blank stare Belial fixed him with shook him to the core.

"You know why I've come and what I must do."

"I've seen the truth," Sardurvial said. "I've seen through your lies and false promises."

Belial's eyes narrowed and his perfect face wrinkled at the forehead and around the mouth. "You've done much for me, Sardurvial, and I wished to do much for you. But, you've transgressed . . ."

"But I've seen it with my own eyes."

"What is it you claimed to have seen?"

"I've seen that the people are really precious."

Belial laughed. "You've got to be kidding me."

"I am not. I've seen what's inside their mind and soul."

Belial held a finger up. "You've seen into the mind and soul of one and claim to know the soul of them all? You're a fool."

"It has made me feel something I've never felt before."

"Like the sleeping child in that other room?" Belial raised a brow. "He is an interesting boy, and like any other child, he can be used to get the things I want."

Sam clenched his fists and took a step towards Belial. "You wouldn't dare!"

Belial smiled and turned his gaze away, then gave Sardurvial his back. "It is you who wouldn't dare."

Sardurvial's strength was nothing compared to Belial's and he knew that.

"Your newfound fondness for the people surprises me, Sardurvial. You were a favorite of Aramus's. He had hopes for you and the role you would play in the final days."

"Well maybe Aramus is trying to fool you and he's like me. Maybe he's decided he will fight for the other side!"

Belial faced Sardurvial. "Aramus is faithful to me, Sardurvial! He doesn't question my word or break the law like you have."

"Well then he is a fool and I shall tell him that!"

Belial took a step back. "Very well. Why don't you tell him for yourself right now?"

Shadows moaned and gathered. They swirled and took shape. Sam understood what was coming for him but could do nothing but wait for it to manifest.

The shadows eventually quieted and melted into the floor leaving Aramus behind. He was a handsome man that stood taller than all of the other fallen. The scar that creased his upper lip complimented his outstanding features like a signature to a portrait, though it remained as a form of punishment.

"I already feel dirty and want to return home," Aramus said. "I feel the filth of this world, these people contaminating my body and mind. But you! You hide among the people because of some silly notion that they aren't responsible for our divide and you dare turn your back on us? On your people and way of life?"

"After what I felt and saw, I must!"

"You risk all of these people's lives!"

"What I do is for the betterment of them."

Aramus looked at Belial and laughed. "So now he's a martyr?" They laughed together. "You dare question the law?"

"There is no law of yours that binds me anymore."

Aramus lunged and grabbed Sardurvial by his shoulders. Sardurvial stiffened and struggled to keep Aramus at arms distance.

"I had to say what I'd come to know," Sardurvial said. "I couldn't deny what I saw and felt. Something inside me has changed."

"What you feel is profane!" Aramus shouted. "You tried to conspire with the group in conference, sway their thoughts to match your own! That is dangerous, Sardurvial. You know the rules, the channels you could've taken to find relief in your time of confusion. We are a civilized community striving for one goal, but we're not civilized to the uncivil. You've upset the others and your actions cannot go unpunished. Quit running from us and take what is coming to you!"

"You dared to tell Belial what we spoke about and break your promise to remain silent! It was never the trees that had ears to carry away our secrets! It was always one of our own looking to benefit off of the confusion and desperate cries of help of the others. I damn you for betraying the secrecy of the group and betraying our trust so that you might gain from it."

Aramus smiled, the crease in his lip kept his mouth a tight slit. "And the others in the group shall be dealt with one at a time once we finish with you!"

Sardurvial felt the sting of the hunt that was to come pain his heart. The others would be blind to the attack and would never receive the chance to seek forgiveness for their misdeeds. To die like that would condemn them to damnation and that was sad because damnation is where they'd all been living and they were too foolish to realize it. What purpose would this have served if that were to be their fate? Sardurvial couldn't accept that. "You've fooled everyone into placing their trust in you and you've used that against them. Their experiences and feelings were to remain ours! You've made false promises and turned your back on your own kind. I can never forgive you for that."

Belial remained in the background, dimmed by the whirling increasing presence of steam that began to fill the room. "It seems we still have some similarities after all Sardurvial. You've betrayed us and the promise you made me after the fall was nothing but a lie!"

Sardurvial reflected on the day he promised Belial he would forever aid him in his crusade. He remembered staring into his distant eyes, so cold and calculating, withdrawn and calloused, pointed at their misfortune and cruel fate. He could feel the love around him, but the moans of the anguished who were rejected and ousted like them were alone and afraid and desperate to have Belial lead them.

And for a long time he did. He built a new society, ranks within an army and strict rules to follow. Those that dared break a law met a brutal fate, thus making everyone obedient to the law they didn't understand. And hidden within that law was a terrible truth Belial tried to conceal from everyone. But Sardurvial discovered that truth.

Sardurvial shook his head. "I was a fool to make any promise to you! If I have to crawl on my hands and knees and beg God for forgiveness, then that is what I'll do."

Belial tittered. "You know you can never return Sardurvial. You are trapped here until we decide to take you."

"I won't give up. I serve the people now."

"Then it is you who is the fool," Aramus growled and with extraordinary strength, shoved Sardurvial. He stumbled backwards and fell into the bathtub.

The shower curtain wrapped his body and the continuing jet of hot water that shot out of the showerhead tightened the curtains hold on him.

"No," Sardurvial shouted, and panic started to close in. He fought to stand but his movement and breathing was being constricted. The thought of Belial using his power to bring the curtain to life awakened his fear. He struggled against the tight hold the nylon had on his body and he tried moving his arms that were compressed to his side. Unable to move, he pushed concealed muscles and tendons away from his upper back, sprouting wings that easily tore the curtain away. The wings, white and pure, pumped once and Sardurvial leapt from the steamy confines of the tub, his adrenaline making him oblivious to the scalding water that blistered his skin.

Sardurvial paused in confusion because Belial and Aramus were gone.

"A distraction?" he said. "No!"

Sardurvial ran to the spare bedroom where he laid Jaiden down for the night. The boy lay beneath the giant heap of covers and his mouth hung open as he sucked in breath. Satisfied the boy was alone, he pulled the door closed and allowed the latch to slip into the striker plate gently.

"What are you up to?" he whispered and looked down the empty hallway. He crouched and tiptoed down the hallway, swinging his gaze to the right as he passed the bathroom, then to the left as he passed Kathy's room. Seeing both rooms were clear, he moved onwards, retracting his wings and pulling them inside. He didn't believe for a moment Belial or Aramus had left him just like that.

He continued to creep forward in search of them. Aramus darted into the hallway and stopped. He mocked Sardurvial with a taunting smile and then ran into the kitchen. Sardurvial sprinted forward, giving chase to Aramus before he could escape into the shadows.

Within the confines of the kitchen, Aramus waited, the same taunting smile spread about his face, and he encouraged Sardurvial on with a wiggling finger. Sardurvial continued his charge knowing full well he might be running into another trap.

Sardurvial hit Aramus with a stiff shoulder and felt a sharp stinging pain deaden his arm. The two tumbled to the floor and rolled about, each one looking to gain the upper hand. Aramus threw a wild punch from his back, connecting heavily with Sardurvial's eye.

Stars filled Sardurvial's head and he was dizzied.

The locks on the front door jiggled, slid back and brought pause to the battle. Sardurvial looked at the door and noticed the chain had been taken off. He twisted within Aramus's grasp and began to fight out of pure desperation.

The door swung open and Kathy stepped inside the apartment. Sardurvial fell to the floor, slapping the linoleum with his palms, knees and the side of his face. Aramus disappeared into the shadows.

Sardurvial remained still, sprawled out on the floor, left to contemplate the reasons why they departed like that.

"Oh my God," Kathy said, and pushed the door closed and hurried to Sardurvial's side. His new clothes were in shreds, and she tended to a red knot that had formed underneath his eye. His body was soaked with sweat and he panted like a lion in the heat of the mid afternoon African sun.

"Sam! Are you all right? What happened?" she said and tried to roll him to his back.

He aided her in her struggle to move him and he remained quiet, concentrating on slowing his breathing.

"Sam," she muttered her concern, her hair dangling in his face. "Say something, are you all right?"

The touch was gentle and it was something he had missed. Her smell was sweet and he liked her being near. He contemplated his next step, knowing he had to tell her his secrets. All of them. And no matter what, he had to tell her everything. She wasn't going to believe his words, he was certain of that, but he was willing to go to great lengths to prove his words were true.

CHAPTER 12

SIDES DRAWN
10,000 BC

Belial marched through the immaculate city streets with a strident and disorderly mass following him. The crowd was destructive, pulling vegetation out of the ground and destroying property while they shouted their purpose proudly. Residents in the big high risers looked out their windows and down from their balconies, trying to make sense of the procession. But the shouting voices were jumbled and hard to discern and their behavior was something appalling and unfamiliar. Some merely watched in disbelief and disgust, while others knowingly flooded the streets and followed the crowd through the city.

On the outskirts of the metropolitan, atop a tall, steep mountain was a lavish home. Always unlocked and welcoming anyone inside, the crowd filed through the front door and flooded the great hallway. Belial continued to lead the people, taking them into the lounge where God sat upon His throne, watching the disorderly gathering move through His home with a confident calm. Observing in silence, everyone found their place and settled.

"Father," Belial said. Disrespect came in the way of a smile and a confident stride as he approached the throne. His calloused heels and long toenails tapped the marble floor.

God searched the crowd then settled his attention on Belial. "Lucifer," He said. "I haven't seen you in a long time."

Belial smiled uneasily. "Call me Belial as everyone else who follows me does. You know how I hate the name you've given me."

God lifted a brow and shifted in His seat. "I do not follow you and the name I've given you is beautiful and it is how I shall address you."

Belial rolled his eyes and huffed his disapproval. "Very well. For now your calling me that will have to do. At the moment there are more pressing matters I've come here to address."

"As to why you've been avoiding me?"

"We've all been avoiding you."

God slid forward in His seat. "I suppose while you're here there are matters of my own that are in need of attention. Shall we start with the reason why you haven't groomed yourself? You look a mess and that isn't how I created you."

Belial bit his lip and shifted his weight from the balls of his feet to the heels. He turned and pointed to those that followed him through the streets and into the lounge. The sea of bodies stretched out the door and seemingly covered every inch of street as far as the eye could see. "You're avoiding the reasons why we've come here now." Belial returned his strong accusing gaze back at the throne. "I speak for all who have followed me here. We are disappointed in you, Lord, myself especially."

Belial paused for reaction. God sunk into His seat relaxed, His attention and composure unwavering.

Belial continued, the hate within tangible through his words. "You have occupied much of your days on the people you've created for the world outside your own and we fear your fondness of them has pulled you away from us forever. You have granted humans gifts on their day of creation that we haven't been granted in the untold eons we've served you. We cannot find reason for this, and I doubt an explanation will do us any good. This obsession you have for the people has gone on for far too long and the gap you've placed between you and your angels has become too great to ever bridge."

Belial bowed his head and shook it in indecision and frustration. There was so much he had to say. Years of pent up frustration and he didn't know where to start. He licked his lips and took a deep breath. Gaining control over his confusion, he spoke with a soft tone. "Why you so desperately search for a way to save them when they are so tainted is something we could never hope to understand. But, what we have come to understand is that we want the same freedom to choose as the people have."

God stood and calmly walked to Belial and settled before him. God towered over him, His expression neither angry nor happy. The crowd took a step back; the air was filled with uncertainty. "What is it you're saying to me, Lucifer?"

Belial reeled. He pushed God, but God remained unmoved. "Damn it!" Belial shouted. "How many times have I asked you to stop calling me that?" Belial stood on his tiptoes, trying to stand eye to eye with God. "And what *we* are saying is that we want to have a chance to raise our throne above yours. We want sovereignty over the earth!"

God searched Belial's eyes for something. Maybe it was hesitation or regret, but whatever it was, He wouldn't find it.

"And what about those that follow you?" God whispered. "Will they validate your words?"

"They will," Belial said unashamed. His voice echoed. "Just ask them!"

God paused then turned away from Belial. He returned to His throne. "No Lucifer, you're right. Everyone that has followed you here has come with the knowledge of what you've done and what you stand for. I can hear their thoughts, feel their disdain." God bowed His head. "This is all a shame, really."

"What is?" Belial growled, his control volatile and unpredictable. "Don't start acting like you care now!"

God sighed and looked at Belial with compassion. "I never stopped caring, not for one moment. You all felt I was distant because I already gave you what you're here seeking now. I gave you freedoms just like the people have. How else could you have come to these decisions? Do you think I would place a thought inside your heads that I no longer cared for all of you? And how could you've decided to find hate in your heart for the people I created in my own image?" God shook his head. "To think you could steal from me without having the freedom of choice is ludicrous."

"You set us up!"

"I did no such thing. I gave you what you wanted because I felt it in your hearts. And now look how you've abused it."

Belial turned to the crowd. "You see, don't you? He set us up!"

"This is a sad day for the Heavens and things will never be the same," God said, and everyone remained tense. "But a revelation has hit me and I have figured a way I could offer the people forgiveness." He pointed at Belial. "It's your hate for the people and your selfish intentions that are responsible for this disclosure. Things will only get worse for you from this day forward because you will see my plan unfolding. You will see it's you and those that have followed you that are indirectly responsible for the way I shall offer the people their forgiveness. In time, I will give you a chance to tempt even me with your ways, Lucifer. But before that day comes, I will grant you ample time to settle into your new role."

Belial contemplated His words. Their meaning held great significance and he would have to consult the Definitive Amassment, the book he stole from the chest inside God's sleeping chambers.

"Damn you and your ways," Belial seethed. "We aren't inferior to you!"

God leaned forward and whispered. "I dare not mention to the others how you will become desperate and turn on your own. That will spoil what will be. When you read the book you stole from me, you will find that I've known this for some time and that this moment was inevitable."

God settled again.

An unsettling wave of displeased shouts that came from outside the lounge quickly worked its way inside. The bodies packed inside the lobby shifted to make room for someone pushing their way through.

"Out of the way, all of you!" a petite, Porcelain Faced woman said. She emerged from the crowd and bowed before the Throne of God. "My Lord."

She turned with a snap, a hardened stare fixed on Belial.

"You dare become arrogant?" she said. "How does one become so brazen when he's been given such a privileged life? You're thankless for the gifts you've received." Porcelain Face turned to face the crowd that disappeared into the hallway and spilled into the streets. She shouted her words. "All of you have! You come here seeking a gift called freewill. Now that you've found you've already been granted it and made terrible choices with it, will you now realize it is no gift at all?" Porcelain Face lowered her voice and returned her attention to Belial. "It is a curse and now you understand how that is so. Why do you think our Lord has been so concerned for the people of the world?"

"Let them burn, I don't care!" Belial said. "Your perfect face and righteous attitude sickens us all Angelina. We will be glad to be away from you and any that is like you!"

Angelina stepped nose-to-nose with Belial and ground her teeth. She talked through tightened lips. "And I will be glad to remind you that you're the one who has made your life a living hell!"

"And you will be there to do so, Angelina," God said. "Now step aside, Angelina, I cast the corrupt out and let it be known they may never return."

God threw His hands out and Belial and everyone that followed him were swept up in a twirling wind and spit out upon the earth. Bodies rained down from the skies, falling into raging seas, crashing into forests throughout the world, and onto hard, barren lands most had never seen before.

CHAPTER 13

THE TRUTH

Sunday, October 16th, 12:22 am

Jaiden sat up and watched the darkness with widened eyes. His heart pounded and his skin was covered in a layer of sweat.

Something had awoken him.

He looked at the closet and the door was closed.

"I mean you no harm," a soft voice said, and Jaiden saw the figure of a man silhouetted in the moonlight that beamed through the sheer white curtains. The figure stood with his arms by his sides, looking out the window.

Fear didn't register with Jaiden and he didn't know any better to question why. He rubbed his eyes and struggled to see who it was that had awoken him. The figure was a tall man and he was thinly built.

"Sam?" Jaiden said. "Is that you?"

The dark figure turned and faced Jaiden. He raised a finger up to his lips. "Shh," he said. "Whisper or they'll hear us."

Jaiden grabbed his covers and pulled them over his head. Those words weren't spoken by Sam! He curled into the fetal position and hugged a pillow. It would provide him with ample protection like it had all those nights in his room. The idea that the monster from his closet had altered its appearance and followed him to his aunt's house made him tremble.

He thought he had escaped it, at the very least, for the night.

Jaiden listened to the sounds around him and he could hear Sam and Kathy talking, but they were far enough away that they were unable to provide him with any protection. If he were to jump from the bed and make a break for the door, the beast made to look like a man would catch him. If he was to make it out of the room, by the time he convinced either his Aunt Kathy or Sam to check the room for the monster it would be long gone.

Jaiden moved the covers away and spied the room. He looked at the window and the glow of the moonlight had faded. And yet the details of the man were somehow decipherable in the thick darkness.

Walking to Jaiden's bed, the man moved in silence, Jaiden's fear replaced by a feeling of comfort. But the feeling receded and came back again like water lapping the shoreline. In one of the moments of fear, he covered himself again, regretting ever having looked a second time.

Sunday, October 16th, 12:47 am

Jaiden's bed creaked and shifted as the dark figure settled on the foot of the bed. He would remain silent to allow the child some time to adjust to his being near. Confident the boy would adapt to his will, he was patient.

The dark figure reached down and carefully pulled the covers back, exposing Jaiden's small, pale foot that dangled out of a baseball pajama bottom. He reached to touch the young smooth skin, but before he was able to appreciate it, Jaiden pulled away and kicked the blankets over his feet.

Fear opened Jaiden up and he pushed trust inside the boy.

"It's okay," the dark figure said with a voice of beauty and care, knowing now was the perfect time to speak. "I'm Sam's friend. I've come from far away looking to help him and I'm hoping you would be willing to help me."

Jaiden was suddenly and unexplainably calmed, his swaying fear snuffed and his curiosity roused.

"It's okay," the dark figure said. "I'm Sam's friend. I've come from far away looking to help him and I'm hoping you'd help me."

The voice he heard was neutral and seeming sincere in the purest way, just like Sam's. He moved the covers away from his eyes and looked at the dark figure that was really just a man.

Jaiden appraised him. The man sat with his head down.

"Would you be willing to do that?" the man said.

"Yes," Jaiden said, and was compelled to reach out and touch the man with the soft, warm flesh. He felt the muscles beneath were hard and it made him feel safe.

"Well that's good to hear because I would do the same for you."

"Do you want me to tell him you're here?"

"No. Not yet. I have to think things through."

"Are you sad?"

"Why don't you lie down and go to sleep? I'm going to stay in your room with you and watch over you while you sleep. I know that terrible creature that lives in your closet has been bothering you. I'll talk to Sam sometime tomorrow and make him aware of it. He'll help me get rid of it. But for tonight I'm going to make sure the closet creature doesn't bother you. Is that okay with you?"

Jaiden smiled and situated himself beneath the covers and sunk into the soft bed. "You're going to protect me?"

"Yes I am."

"I like that," Jaiden said.

"Goodnight Jaiden," the man said. He stood and walked over to the window and looked outside. The clouds drifted, making way for the glow of the moon again. The light illuminated the man with the clef lip, and he turned to watch the child that had already begun to fall asleep.

Saturday, October 15, 11:57 pm

Sam held a washcloth filled with ice to his swollen bloody lip. His elbows were on the tabletop and his forehead rested in the palms of his hands. The new shirt and pants he wore were torn and coated with blotches of dried blood and stained with sweat.

Kathy stood inside the kitchen preparing hot tea, her back to Sam.

"I think I should call the cops and file a report," she said.

"That won't do either of us any good," Sam said.

She poured steaming water into coffee cups and fetched two tea bags, dunking them into the water.

"Who was the man you were fighting with?"

"His name is Aramus."

"And he came into my home without breaking in?"

Sam nodded. "That's what I said."

"And you also said he disappeared while I was unlocking the door and entering the house. That doesn't make much sense."

"No, I couldn't see how it would. I need you to understand that is what happened," he said. "Sit down so I can help you understand."

Kathy turned and faced Sam, her eyes filled with tears. "I don't know why, but I'm afraid of what you have to say."

"You need to know what you're involved in. I want to tell you what I was running from when you first found me."

Kathy wiped her eyes and scooped sugar into the cups of tea.

"This is crazy," she said, and poured milk into the glasses and took her time to clean up before she moved to the table where Sam sat with the dripping washcloth. She placed a cup of tea in front of him and struggled with back pain as she eased into the chair on the opposite side of the table. Her empty gaze shifted around nervously and found Sam watching her. She clasped both hands around the mug and blew on the steaming hot tea.

"Are you okay?" Sam said.

Kathy nodded.

Sam pulled the washcloth away from his mouth and the bleeding stopped. "I want you to know that what I'm about to tell you is going to be hard for you to believe, but I will prove that what I have to say is the truth. I can no longer allow you to be fooled by my silent command to manipulate your mind. I am confused and concerned by the actions of my enemy. They're becoming reckless."

"Who are they Sam?"

"Yesterday when you found me in the stairwell, I really found you."

"What?"

"Although I had no intention of involving anyone else in this, especially a human, I was desperate and fearful for my life. I had hoped, if I was going to die, that I would do so in peace. Not that I deserved it because I had done some terrible things in my life."

"Terrible things?" She stared at him. "Like what Sam?"

"I know once I tell you, the look in your eyes as you judge me is going to kill me inside."

"I won't judge you."

"Yes, you will," Sam said. "Because I will let go of the hold I've had on your emotions since I met you. What I've done is reprehensible. Don't you find it odd that you've made some irrational decisions you normally wouldn't have made?"

"Every decision I've made has been my own."

"No, it hasn't. You would never allow a stranger in your house the way you did me."

Kathy stared.

"Or allow me to watch over your nephew when you really know nothing about me."

Kathy stared at Sam, wordless.

"In a place so far away from here yet so close its secrets are tangible to all the people of this world, is the world where I come from. It's a place of false promises and silent despair. It's a miserable soul-less place that's an incurable cancerous tumor that infiltrates the world. You know what Hell is Kathy, but don't think there are deformed creatures with spiked tails and fire red skin holding forks torturing the damned. That's a severe misconception brought forth by ancient fables. As you can see, we appear to be like you with subtle differences. We are stronger, much stronger, and along with our great strength we posses supernatural abilities beyond your imagination. We can fly and manipulate with the power of suggestion."

"Is that what you've done to me?" she said.

Sam looked away in shame. "It is."

"Why would you?"

"Corruption is all I know. I manipulate and lie and care nothing about people and their suffering."

"Why?"

"Because we didn't believe we had anything good. So we created our own reality and built a structural paradise. We made them from marble and inlaid them with gold. Every inch of flooring was covered with the hide of every great beast that roamed the earth. We crammed every home we created with items of luxury. But there was one thing we couldn't possess. It was something you were able to feel every day without thought and that is love."

Kathy sat up straight, his words stung. "Mine was torn away."

"And I threw mine away."

"I'm sorry," she said.

"So am I."

She leaned back in the chair and slid the mug of tea around the table, fighting a quivering lip.

"I now know we were fools because we willingly turned away from the best kind of love anyone could ever hope to have."

She took a sip and kept her gaze over the rim of the cup. "I would give anything to have Rocco back again."

"I know you would. I can feel the void that your loss has left inside you and it is terrible."

A tear fell from her eye and she looked away. She straightened her back and cringed at the ache.

"I know how bad the pain is in your back, Kathy. It's stabbing you, putting you in agony," Sam said. "When I search your body, I can feel that, too. I wonder why you don't scream out and submit to the pain?"

"Because I have to believe I am stronger than the pain. I have to carry on."

He studied Kathy for a moment and resigned to his thoughts with a smile.

"The truth," he said, and tensed the muscles in his shoulders and pushed outwards. White feathery wings sprouted out of his back and wafted the air.

Kathy flinched and groaned. The chair she sat in tipped and spilt her onto the hard floor. A wave of pain overpowered her fear and paralyzed her.

Sam folded his wings away and moved to her side. He placed his hands on her and muttered something indecipherable. Pulling her to her feet, she stood motionless as she watched Sam walk back to his seat and sit.

"Your pain should be gone," he said. "I cannot take it away permanently, but at least I can offer you a reprieve."

She moved, testing what she felt.

"I'm an Angel fallen from the good grace of God. And Belial, the man you've dreamt about, is Lucifer. The devil. I believed his lies the very moment it was introduced to me in the Heavens and I blindly followed his crusade ever since. Today I'm being hunted because I've turned my back on his cause. I broke law, rebelled against his authority and rejected his lies. I discovered the people I'd blamed for my fate and tried to ruin are really precious creatures with hard lives that don't need my kind interfering."

"I don't understand what is happening," Kathy whimpered.

"I am ashamed to say I didn't discover this on purpose or even because I cared. I stumbled on this by accident because I blatantly broke one of Belial's laws. Laws that I have willingly followed since the day we fell."

"You . . . You're a demon?"

"I'm a fallen Angel."

Kathy scooted away.

"I told you that you would judge me. The way you're looking at me right now is unbearable. But please understand that I am no longer what I once was."

Those words stilled her.

"Your cold . . ."

"Is gone," she said. "And my back . . ."

"It's only temporary," he said, and reached for her. He helped her into the seat at the table.

"These events that forced me into hiding started just a few days ago when I was ordered by Belial to influence a bad man. I was to influence him to commit a heinous act that would guarantee his corrupted soul an eternity in damnation with us. We want to ruin the lives of the people because it is them we've always blamed for our fall from grace. It is, at least in our eyes, the people's gifts and their special care that is responsible for our misery."

"How is that our fault?"

"Because you existed."

"Our lives can be Hell."

"I didn't know that at the time. We felt like we were being neglected and cheated by God. We weren't given the same freedoms and love the people were given."

"Is it true? Were you being neglected?"

"No, of course it wasn't true. But that didn't stop us from using it as an excuse to make our stand against Him. I remember when Belial went before the throne and told God what we thought about the people and he insisted we wanted out of Heaven."

Sam shook his head and laughed.

"I was so damn proud of Belial and was expecting something so much different than what happened. God seemed genuinely sad, but Belial continued to yell about His preferential treatment of the people. He accused Him of treating them better than the angels and how we needed to be freethinkers." Sam slapped the table and resigned with a laugh. "Freethinkers! How blind could we be? We already had that and didn't even know it. How else could we have chosen to stand against God? When we finally knew the price of freewill, it was too late. We were going to be judged for our actions just as the people of the world were. We learned that is the price of freewill. In that moment, I realized I made a terrible error but my pride got in the way and I wouldn't dare say it. That is when Angelina came forward. She is the Angel with the perfect faith and a face like porcelain."

Kathy gasped. "I think I've seen her!"

Sam stood. "You have? Where?"

"At the hospital. She told me how my strength and courage was being tested. Tonight she was there and told me how you were in danger and that I needed to wake you. She's the reason I called you."

"I am saved!" Sam said, and a tear fell from his eye. He sat. "I am certain they have come to assist me because they recognize the good in what I'm trying to do."

Kathy reached across the table and squeezed Sam's hands.

"I was sent to influence a man named Lenny," Sam said. "His sinful acts were mine to concoct. But before I could devise a plan, I needed to study him. I spent days watching him and I realized I never met someone so strange. During the day he functioned like an average anybody. He would get up at seven in the morning, start the coffee, grab the paper and enjoy some breakfast. But he wasn't just an average anybody. Twisted thoughts whirled within his mind as he read about detailed crimes headlining the newspaper. Often times he wished it were him that was doing the crimes and wanted to be feared. He was a coward and I just needed to encourage him to do it.

"Day after day I studied him. I followed him into the bathroom in an attempt to study every aspect of his habits. He would make the water in the shower so hot he would barely be able to stand underneath the spray. Getting into the shower was a ritual that was carried out day after day. I would sit there, blind to his eyes, mesmerized by his compulsions. He would turn his back to the scolding hot water and back in, grunting and groaning, tolerating the pain, almost relishing in it.

"He did that because his parents had beaten him every day of his adolescent life and he had grown accustomed to it. He was often locked in a closet and became friends with the darkness around him. It was the only thing that gave him peace.

"I mulled over my plans while Lenny kept his head down and clamped his eyes shut as the scalding hot water washed over him. He never used soap, and after his shower was done, the pungent smell of his body dulled but never left. After his shower, he would get into his car and drive to work: Sam's Market."

"Sam's Market?" Kathy said. "I shop there."

"I know," Sam said. "I think I've seen you there. Lenny might have assisted you a few times."

Kathy shivered.

"Lenny worked in the refrigerated aisle and would do his eight hours with passion and precision. There was never a complaint about him or his work. He was a stellar employee and the perfect candidate to help us make the innocent pay for their humanity."

Kathy shook her head. "I can't believe what I'm hearing."

"Once Lenny's shift was up," Sam said. "He would punch his timecard and head home. He would always go out of his way to pass by the local high school. At first I thought it was simple curiosity. The way he would look at the kids was with a dangerous craving that could barely be contained.

"I'd been sitting in the backseat of Lenny's car, my feet were up on the seat and I was blissful knowing what I was about to do when I spotted her. I had come to know her as Redhead. She was the perfect victim for Lenny and I told him that day I first spotted her. His eyes searched the crowd of kids hungrily, the direction I gave him unspecific. But when he located her, I knew I had him. I rubbed my hands with delight; I would plunge Lenny's soul into the same hell I had to suffer and I would send the girl there along with him. When Lenny's eyes locked onto Redhead, his heart thundered with a yearning that needed to be fulfilled and shared immediately."

"I don't want to hear this anymore," Kathy said. "I don't want to know what happened to that girl."

"You must know what I once was."

"No," Kathy said and shook her head. She covered her ears and clamped her eyes shut.

"Put your hands on the table, I have to tell my story," Sam said, and Kathy's hands were forced away from her ears by something unseen and placed on the table. She couldn't move them and whimpered.

"I told Lenny her name was Redhead, and he wanted to take her that very moment. But his lust made him careless."

"Why would you do this to someone so young? Someone so undeserving?"

"Because it was what I was."

Kathy sobbed. "It seems so senseless."

"I demanded he listen to me and I told him no, that he wasn't to do anything yet."

Kathy breathed a sigh of relief. "Thank god."

"Only because I wanted him to do it right. My way."

Her eyes went wide. "You are a monster!"

"The worst kind," he said, the sadness within profound. "In that moment, Lenny drove along, his neck twisting as he watched Redhead until she was out of sight. I laughed in delight knowing they would be the perfect match."

"I can't do this," she said and began to weep. "I can't sit here and listen to this."

"Kathy, I need you to look at me."

"I can't."

"Please."

She looked at him with tears streaming down her cheeks.

"I was always in control of my chosen victim. I'd done this type of thing so many times that I didn't have to think about it, but there was a rule to never watch your chosen agent killing the victim. I never thought to break the rule because it didn't seem important enough. But when Redhead came along, I found she was the very first victim I'd gained any interest in. She had a matchless appreciation for life. To her the breeze seemed a little cooler, the sun a little brighter, and the day just a little longer."

Sardurvial's eyes were glazed, rife with tears.

"For days Lenny and I watched Redhead together, my presence was accepted in his mind as if it had always been there. I instructed Lenny every step of the way. I told him about the equipment he would need, about the precautions he would have to take in order to keep himself from getting caught. I intended to keep on using him throughout his entire life to provide us with dozens of souls.

"Then the day came when we went into the forest that Redhead had used to get home from school every day. The manmade path was thin and sinuous, providing cover for Lenny. When she started on the path, I told Lenny to dig in, and he nestled his chubby body into the greenery.

"I could feel the building tension as Redhead walked right by Lenny without a clue he was near. When I gave him the order to attack, I was swimming in a sea of euphoria.

"He caught her and tied and bound her. Of course she fought him and made the mistake of turning around and looking at him. And when she did, everything suddenly turned very serious and dark. It was a darkness that frightened even me. I realized then that I should have left, but something kept me there. Whatever it was remained unseen and it was paralyzing.

"I watched Lenny draw back the broken pistol he carried and strike Redhead on top of her head. I was stunned by the mimicking stinging I felt on top of my head. Dizzied, I teetered helplessly and fell to my knees. I watched in slow motion as Redhead slumped forward and fall to the ground. Her thoughts spiraled out of control and before I could make sense of it, years of her memory containing both pleasure and pain flashed before my eyes. I gasped with her, sharing in her pain and experiences of life, unable to resist its overpowering invasion within my psyche. I wanted to scream at Lenny, to make him stop, but I couldn't utter a single word; my consciousness was fading. I collapsed to my side and found myself lying beside Redhead. I watched the blood pour from the gaping wound on her head. And as I looked at it, I couldn't help but think how that was my fault. My awareness like the anger I held towards the people began to leave me. And as I lay on the pathway inside the forest, I drifted into a state of unconsciousness.

"When I finally awoke, night had fallen. My body ached and I was sickened by the memories of Redheads suffering. I struggled to my feet and started to run. I could still feel Redheads fear—see brief glimpses of her current situation. I opened my wings and took to flight. Pumping my wings without pause and with a fierce intensity, I set out to undo what I had done. But I could feel cold hands wrapping my neck and I struggled to breathe. I knew Lenny was killing her by suffocation and I was experiencing that attack."

"Please tell me you saved her," Kathy said.

"Redhead was losing her will to live and Lenny's rage had grown to a boil. She gurgled underneath the tight grip Lenny had around her throat and sputtered, her lips flapping, throwing spit in thick wads up into the air that rained down on her face."

Sam released a quivering sigh and took a deep breath.

"Oh no," Kathy said. "Why would you want me to know this?"

"Because someone that was caring needed to know how she died. Someone like you that could mourn her."

Kathy sobbed.

"Her soul was ripped from her body and it has carried the wounds Lenny had inflicted upon her. She struggled to breathe and dropped to her knees, unable to find relief from the horrible acts committed against her. I could see her fear as Lenny hovered over her body. Strangely, he cried and wiped the spit from her face with hands that trembled. He pled for forgiveness, and he pulled her body close, holding it tight.

"When I arrived at Lenny's house, I crashed through the basement door. I lashed out and grabbed the frail man by his neck and squeezed him the way he had squeezed the girl. The tendons and his windpipe cracked underneath the power of my grip and his body went limp. I tossed his body aside as if it were a piece of trash. I killed a human with my own hands and didn't care if God sent his Angels for me. I needed to rid the world of that evil.

"I walked to Redhead's body and closed her eyelids with the tender brush of my hand. And there I sat, at the foot of the bed and cried for hours, realizing why Belial made it a rule to never watch our victims die. Their pain and suffering becomes ours, and the pain surrounding a violent death is unmerciful and haunting and it never leaves us alone."

CHAPTER 14

SECRETS

Sunday, October 16th, 12:17 am

Sam paused to sip from his cooling cup of tea. Kathy remained seated at the table across from him, her eyes wandered aimlessly while her mind pondered Sam's captivating tale. It was a tragic story yet so fascinating. If she hadn't felt the change in her body when he spoke those foreign words and saw wings sprout from his back, she wouldn't believe it. Yet there was also something very believable about anything spoken from his lips. It was as if his words were absolute and irrefutable. The very first moment he came into Kathy's life, this was the way it had been and she suddenly understood that he had been controlling her in some way. At first she didn't want to believe it, now she couldn't deny it.

An apprehensive feeling invaded her comfort and she shifted around. Did he give up some control and that was why she was increasingly becoming uneasy or did he still have some power over her? She identified it as a presence lurking within her mind and she searched for it, but it was elusive and possibly imagined.

"After I calmed and gathered myself," Sam said, unbroken from his last thought, interrupting Kathy's, "I reluctantly left Redhead alone in that dismal basement and returned home, to Hell.

Though apprehensive to do so, I knew I must. I tried to repress my adverse feelings but knew full well I couldn't keep up the facade for very long. The others would know. They would sense the difference within me and I knew it was just a matter of time before I was discovered."

"Then why would you return? Why not stay away?"

"Because I had to go back. If I didn't, then they would know I had broken the law. And if I went back, then maybe I could find someone else that had a similar experience."

"You were discovered," she said. "That's why you were in the stairwell."

"You're jumping ahead," Sam said. "What happened in between is important."

Sardurvial had changed and could never revert back to what he was before he met Redhead and Lenny. Anger coursed through his body and he despised everything the people of Sheol stood for. But he had to conceal it because if he were to be discovered, he would be put to death and what purpose would all of this have served?

The Fallen roamed the streets, some with purpose and others without. All that occupied the city marched with great strength and pride and acknowledged their fellow brother, nodding and saying hello as he passed them by. He returned the good gesture no matter how fake the exchange really was, and pressed onwards, heading to the temple where Belial always stayed. It was where he ordered his minions to carry out his plans.

The temple was brilliant, a masterpiece to awe the city people. Perfectly squared walls capped with a golden dome and a giant interior that was mazelike, but Sardurvial knew his way and came upon Belial in the steam room. The steam emanated from the bubbling water and Belial floated around on a raft. His eyes were closed, legs crossed and his arms were behind his head.

"Hello Belial," Sardurvial said.

"Sardurvial?" Belial said and cracked his eyes open. Tense moments passed before he revealed a pleased smile at Sardurvial.

Sardurvial found a stone bench facing the pool and sat. The rock was as hot as coal. "You'd gotten word about my mission's success?"

"Look at yourself . . ."

At the request of Belial, Sardurvial appraised himself. His hands were covered with dried blood and so were his clothes. Crimson splatters made a colossal portrait of tragedy.

"You got inside his head? Influenced him to do our bidding?" Belial said, and paddled the water, guiding his raft towards Sardurvial. "How did it go?"

"As planned," Sardurvial said. "Lenny is dead as is the girl."

"The girl?" Belial said, his smile gone and his eyes wide with the question.

"A Redhead girl filled with dreams and aspirations. She was the perfect victim, the perfect soul for us to gain control over before it could find its way into the Heavens."

Belial pondered Sardurvial's words and his confusion didn't clear. "The girl never came through."

"That's odd," Sardurvial said, but knew why. The girl was pure and she didn't waver—even as she looked into death's eyes and was asked to denounce her love of God. "The man named Lenny?"

Belial's smile returned. "Ah yes, Lenny! He's a mean bastard. Although he's not cooperating, he's being cleaned up and prepared as we speak. He will learn his place soon enough."

"Very good," Sardurvial said, smiling with delight, playing the part.

"Are you pleased enough with your work that you'd like to share your experience?"

"I am beyond pleased, Belial," Sardurvial said, and pushed away his smile and stood. He stepped to the pool's edge and squatted before Belial in an attempt to intensify the experience he was about to share. "I grew quite fond of Lenny. During the few days I spent with him I got to learn what you'd noticed from this room. He's demented and I thought he would serve the cause well so I returned for him after he finished the girl. I was excited by what I saw and couldn't control myself. His death was beautiful!"

Belial chuckled, looked at the bloodstains covering Sardurvial and traced them with a wet finger. "Although I didn't order you to kill, you make me proud. You need to be more careful or they might take notice."

"Who cares? Let them come!"

Belial laughed and motioned Sardurvial forward. "Come into my pool and clean yourself off."

Without hesitation Sardurvial stood and walked to the stairs. Step by step he descended into the boiling water, fighting off the agonizing sting that started at his feet and climbed up his body the deeper he submerged himself into the water.

Submerged up to his neck, he waded to Belial. Once beside the raft, he took hold of Belial's hand

and kissed it. "Thank you. Your offering humbles me and I don't know what to say."

"You've done well Sardurvial and you've earned rest. Aramus requested you meet with him at the tavern. Take the night off and go see him, but be sure you look presentable before you go; you're one of the elite and you have an image to uphold."

Sardurvial smiled at Belial, bowed, turned and treaded the water to the stairs. The stinging had melded into numbness and the blood that stained his skin had been boiled away.

Once out of the pool, he returned to his quarters and changed his clothes. The feeling in his body slowly returned and he hurried off to the tavern in search of Aramus. Pushing open the swinging wooden saloon style doors, he was greeted with the hectic bustle of the taverns innards. The jukebox was blaring and a crowd of men hooted at naked women dancing on elevated platforms. Stalls all around the bar was horseshoe shaped, and Sardurvial pushed himself through the thick crowd. He found Aramus sitting alone, hugging a foamed up beer at the round table that they'd long ago claimed as being theirs.

"Aramus," Sardurvial said, and his head rose up and a delighted smile spread across his face. Aramus stood and embraced Sardurvial with a long, loving hug.

"It is good to see you, friend."

"It is good to see you, too," Sardurvial said, and patted his back, breaking away from the hug.

"You're late," Aramus said. "I was beginning to worry. The others have already gone to the trees. We should leave now, they're waiting."

Aramus took a long gulp of beer and they set off to the forest on the outskirts of town. The location remained secreted to five members of the elite that remained close since the fall. When they emerged into the small clearing, Jesseth paced the ground with his hands interlocked behind his back and his feet kicking fallen sticks and small rocks. The sword and sheath resting on his hip swung with each step he took. Ishmael lay across a fallen limb looking into the cloudless sky partly obscured by the grouped tree-tops, mulling over some private thought. Abraham stroked his beard, watching the forest. Aramus stepped on a stick that cracked loudly underfoot and gained his attention.

"Aramus! Sardurvial!" Abraham cheered, and sprang forward. "It's good to see you chaps. I thought we were going to have to start without you! We all have much to share so let's get on with it."

Jesseth pulled his sword out of the leather sheath and rested its tip in the ground. He leaned his fore-arms on the stately steel handle and clapped his hands. Ishmael sat up abruptly and rubbed his eyes and gave a mighty yawn.

"I've been looking forward to this for a long time," Jesseth said. "And I'm sure we all have plenty of things to share this day."

Sardurvial put his arm around Jesseth and pulled him close. "I hope to hear something interesting."

The group gathered around in a tight circle.

"I elect Sardurvial," Jesseth said.

"I shouldn't," Sardurvial said.

"He was late and I'd like to know why."

"We shouldn't discuss that," Sardurvial said.

"Aye," Abraham said. "Your reluctance makes us more interested."

"It shouldn't. Not this," Sardurvial said.

"Come on out with it," Ishmael said. "Quit stalling."

"Let's put it to vote," Jesseth said. "All in favor say I."

"I," the group said together, voting unanimously.

Sardurvial shook his head. "I'm telling you, someone else should go. Leave this alone."

Abraham playfully shoved Sardurvial into the circle. "Speak up, you have us all wanting to know."

Sardurvial licked his lips, looked around nervously, and then settled. "I met a girl and nicknamed her Redhead."

"Aye," Abraham said.

"And I met a man and his name was Lenny. He was something worse than I have ever seen. I had him kill her and I didn't leave."

"You what?" Ishmael said.

"I didn't leave. I watched the whole thing and experienced everything she did and it was terrible."

Stunned, the group looked at Sardurvial.

"I feel her pain, see her face, smell her hair every single second since she was killed and it won't leave me alone."

Abraham stepped forward, his full beard covering his face and hanging on his chest. Behind the thick cover of hair his eyes were sad.

"Aye, I've seen something terrible and I want to share it too, Sardurvial. But, I hadn't the nerve to say so before this moment, even to you guys for fear of punishment. Aramus's warnings about the trees being alive, having ears and looking to steal our secrets away scared me to death."

Abraham looked at the trees all around and above. He looked back at Sardurvial.

"What if it were true? What if they could pass our secrets along to the wind that would carry it to Belial? But I guess it doesn't matter now, does it? If they can hear us and carry along our secrets, then I wouldn't want you to get punished alone for speaking out because I broke the law, too. I witnessed the death and felt the pain of one of my victims like you and I regret ever having done so. It was a long time ago and I've worked hard to ignore it. I no longer wish to do the people harm."

"Does it get any better?" Sardurvial said. "The feelings and visions?"

Abraham shook his head. "No."

Jesseth pulled at his chin and stared into the gleam of his sword. Aramus stared at Abraham and Sardurvial with disdain and disbelief but it went unnoticed.

Jesseth pulled his sword out of the ground and let it rest deep in its sheath. He approached Sardurvial in the center of the circle, his expression filled with anger.

"Do you want to know what I experienced?" Jesseth said, his jaw quivering.

"From the look in your eyes, I'd say I do," Sardurvial said.

"Aye," Abraham said.

Jesseth's face contorted, fitting his rage. "I felt the pain of my victim before and after he died. But you know what?"

Sardurvial raised his brow and Jesseth removed his sword from its sheath, lifted it over his head and pulled it downwards, chopping a mound of dirt.

"I had to cut off his head because the person I tempted wouldn't kill him. He wanted to see him suffer and I couldn't take the pain of his suffering anymore! I can still hear the screams, feel the fear . . ."

Jesseth moistened his lips and stared at the ground.

"Argh!" he shouted, and spun with his sword and tossed it. It flew through the air and sunk into the ground some twenty yards from where the group stood. It wobbled as its blade settled almost halfway into the soil. "I hate what I've done!"

He panted like a wild animal.

"I sat over the body for hours, waiting for God to send His Angels to punish me for laying a hand on His people. But He never did and I couldn't figure out why."

"I did the same thing and God didn't send anyone after me either," Sardurvial said.

"I was curious to know why Belial had made such a rule," Ishmael said. "Something tempted me to find out what it was, so like all of you, I stuck around to see. I saw what you all saw and felt what you did. I had a victim I had to kill as well and I waited for the Angels to come for me. But they never did. I haven't been able to shake the feeling of their suffering, and it has slowly been driving me mad, I swear it. We should leave here and try to ascend to the Heavens and beg for forgiveness. Maybe God will have mercy on us."

Ishmael started to sob. His shoulders bounced and his fingers went up to his eyes and pinched the bridge of his nose.

"What is this?" Aramus said, outraged. "An elite crying? You all start openly speaking about stories of woe and how you've broken the law?" His anger, like the sorrow of the group, was intense.

"Aye, lower your voice Aramus or you'll expose us!' Abraham said.

"I'll not be silent when it comes to law and the elite crossing that line!" Aramus said, his words at a shout. "What you all are talking about is nonsense, and I will not allow it! How could you speak of ascending to the Heavens? Where is your allegiance?"

"We are all still here. We're talking about it, that's all."

"I'll tell Belial about this conversation and allow him to deal with you. The rule he made to never witness a death was placed there for a reason and now you know why! His thinking is beyond our understanding."

Jesseth grabbed Aramus's shoulder and spun him around. "You'll tell Belial nothing Aramus. We have a pact!"

Aramus pushed Jesseth. "Not anymore. This wasn't the purpose of our gathering here, it never was. Sardurvial should've known better than to share something like this with the group. Look at what he's caused."

"I told you it wasn't a good idea!"

"No, it wasn't and you should have known better to keep it to yourself!"

"I couldn't help it, I'm confused by what I felt," Sardurvial said.

"You're a criminal!" Aramus said.

Jesseth shoved Aramus back and he staggered. Aramus regained his composure and charged Jesseth with a scream accompanying his assault. The two collided and wrestled on their feet, pushing and shoving, grabbing at each other's clothes. Abraham and Ishmael ran in and worked on pulling Jesseth from the entanglement, and without hesitation Sardurvial grabbed Aramus and worked to free him.

"Calm down, my friend. We can work this out," Sardurvial said to Aramus. "We just need a moment to cool down."

"I don't need a moment," Aramus said. He turned and threw a wild punch. It was telegraphed and grossly slow. He was off balance and Sardurvial ducked the punch. Responding, Sardurvial came up and delivered a punch of his own that caught Aramus on the mouth.

A meaty *thock* sound stopped everyone and Aramus toppled over, blood spraying the air and staining the ground with thick droplets. Sardurvial shook his hand in an attempt to rid his knuckles of the stinging.

Dizzied, Aramus shook his head and struggled to his knees. He attempted to stand but couldn't so he settled on his laurels. His lip was split all the way up to his nose. Thick red blood painted his face and soaked his shirt as far down as the middle of his chest.

"Kill me now and bury me in this forest because if I get out of here, Belial is going to find out about this!" Aramus said.

"Aye, no one is going to kill you Aramus. You are part of the brotherhood."

"I've already told you there is no more brotherhood. You've all admitted to breaking the law."

"Please, Aramus, things got way out of hand just now," Ishmael said. "You need to think this through before you run to Belial and tell him what has been discussed here today. This secret confessional group we've assembled is against the law too, and you're telling him what we spoke about incriminates you, too."

Aramus licked his lip and dipped his finger into the wound. He studied the blood on his finger tip and thought silently. "And what about this?" He cocked his head back to allow everyone a better look at the wound Sardurvial had inflicted.

Sardurvial studied it. "It's simple. We return to Belial now and tell him after we had a few beers at the tavern we all went and stole some horses. Drunkenly we rode about, tormenting the dumb animals, and you got thrown."

"And you believe Belial will buy that?" Aramus said, a lisp already evident.

"Aye Aramus, we've got to stick together," Abraham said.

"I," Jesseth said.

"I," Ishmael said.

"I," Sardurvial said. "We stick together no matter what."

"It's such a simple story, it's easily believable," Jesseth said.

"Now stand," Abraham said and offered him his hand.

Jesseth retrieved his sword and placed it in its sheath. As a group, they returned to the temple to tell their story to Belial. On the way, they worked in the details of the story so there were no discrepancies. They recited their parts to be sure there wouldn't be any contradictions.

"Thrown from a horse?" Belial said.

"We were drinking at the tavern," Aramus said. "We had too many."

"I would say."

"Aye," Abraham said. "It was my idea to take the horses."

Belial studied the group. "As punishment for the carelessness of the group, I'm going to allow that scar on Aramus's upper lip to remain. It will serve as a reminder to be more careful and to strive for perfection. Imperfect things make simple, careless mistakes. And all of you, my chosen elite are anything but imperfect. Do you all understand that?"

"We do," the group said, standing at the poolside in the steam room.

"Aramus?"

"Yes Belial?"

"You do understand, don't you?"

"I do."

"Good. You're all dismissed."

Belial paddled away.

"Aramus? I'd like you to stay behind for a moment. I would like to have a word with you in private."

CHAPTER 15

THE OTHER TRUTH

The Past

"What really happened Aramus?" Belial said. The steam added tension, concealing his features. "I don't want to hear anything about a horse. I expect more from you."

Aramus wiped sweat off his brow. "They broke the law. All of them watched their chosen die and experienced their pain. They're all harboring their feelings and I'm afraid that includes them feeling the need to flee before they are discovered."

"As difficult as that is to hear, I appreciate the truth Aramus. Have they mentioned where they're thinking about fleeing to?"

"To the Heavens. They want to go there and beg for forgiveness and seek immunity for their crimes."

Belial remained on his raft and floated on top of the boiling water. "It is impossible for a fallen to return to the Heavens."

"I know that."

"They are desperate and know they are doomed."

"I think examples need to be made to prevent any further dissention."

"Agreed," Belial said. "I need a moment alone to reflect on our conversation. I want you to wait outside for me and once I reach a decision on what we should do, I'll call for you."

Aramus bowed. "As you wish, but we should hurry if we are to stop them."

Once Aramus departed, Belial allowed his body to sink into the air filled raft. He lay motionless in a state of bliss and enjoyed a private laugh.

Feeling Aramus' fear as he picked him out of the group was empowering. He knew why his servant was so scared and for good reason. The events that were now playing out were put into motion a long time ago. It was a glorious moment knowing that the countdown to end time had begun. And the cost that would be paid would be a small price. One elite.

"Just one," he said.

Belial unfolded torn crumbled pages he'd been studying for centuries. The gold foil that once covered the pages had since flaked away. Though it was old in a sense, in another sense it was a timeless treasure. Without hurry, Belial scanned the writing on the pages and couldn't help but acknowledge the meticulous concern that was put into every entry. Every log within was easily and perfectly understandable. No room for question.

"Thank you for all your hard work," he said while looking heavenward. "It will all go to good use."

Belial remembered the day he stumbled on the significant writing. It was the complete listing of each human and Angel alike, both the living and the dead, telling what side each individual would be on during the final war. Heaven and Hell. It was all there, in black and white.

The day he opened that chest and saw the books gleam, opened its cover and saw its writings, Belial knew the value of the information he had at his disposal and the advantages he had gained. He knew he had to keep the book to himself and use its information to better his rule, secure his power, and use it to remove God from the Heavens.

There were five names in particular that he decided to concentrate on. Out of billions, Jesseth, Abraham, Aramus, Ishmael and Sardurvial were the ones that interested him the most. What better statement to make than using those who stood closest to you? As they should, they were going to have a hand in elevating him to the leader of his people. And, in turn, they would be rewarded in kind. One martyred, the others celebrated. But these were secrets that couldn't be revealed yet because the plan was still unfolding.

The five elite warriors closest to the fallen prince will dissent and side with the Heavens.

It was a bold statement written by the hand of God. He planned to change what the ancient book said and ultimately change the Word of God. In order to do that he knew each individual he singled out would have his own part to play in the grand scheme. Some parts were smaller than others, but all were equally important to achieve the result that worked in his favor.

"It will work," he said.

He was confident he molded the five to his will, to make them react exactly as he'd planned them to. He knew their strengths and weaknesses, and understood what they favored and what they would condemn. The day's events proved him completely accurate thus far. His assessment of the players and what they needed to do when he initially began devising his strategy on how to change what had been written in the *Definitive Amassment* was perfect.

"The Definitive Amassment," Belial muttered, and then shouted, "You think you're so infallible that you can put this in writing and think it'll go unchallenged and unchanged?" He settled some, the beat of his heart fast from excitement. "Perhaps creating such a powerful document was your first and last mistake in this war, Lord."

Belial hopped off his raft, treaded the scalding hot water without reacting to its bite. He dressed and made his way to Aramus standing outside his temple. "Gather the townspeople, Aramus, and prepare them for a manhunt. We have four members of our society who've chosen to dissent and they must pay for breaking our law."

CHAPTER 16

RUN FOR YOUR LIFE

Present Day

Sardurvial, Ishmael, Abraham and Jesseth walked the mazelike hallways out of the temple acting casual as not to draw any attention to themselves. When they spoke, they used hushed voices.

"Be ready for anything," Sardurvial said. "I'm not sure if we sold that story about Aramus being thrown from a horse to Belial."

"I don't think we did," Ishmael said. "I was watching Belial and he was nodding to appease us and he kept Aramus behind to get the truth out of him."

"He just may do that," Jesseth said. "Aramus will break."

"I can still feel Redhead's suffering right now and I just want to get away from it. I don't know how much longer I can keep up this facade."

"You'll do it for as long as you'll need to," Jesseth said. "It's about survival now."

"Aye, I think it best we keep quiet until we get to the clearing in the forest," Abraham said. "I don't trust that we are in the clear and ears could be anywhere."

"I agree," Sardurvial said. "Although that girl's suffering ails me, I see no value dying now. We have work to do."

"This moment, what we are going through reminds me of the time when we observed those two dissenters talking in the unexplored southern region of the forest," Ishmael said. "Remember how we stalked them because we were sent to bring them back to Belial so they could face sentencing?"

"Aye, I don't like being reminded of that right now, Ishmael."

"Maybe we should remember it, learn from their mistakes," Sardurvial said.

"My point exactly," Ishmael said.

"Keep quiet everyone," Jesseth said. "I think we should take Abraham's advice and wait until we get into the cover of the forest."

In silence the group moved through the city of Sheol and to the outskirts of town where the forest sat. Once they reached the small clearing, Sardurvial stood in the center of the group.

"We should leave immediately," Sardurvial said. "Something doesn't feel right to me."

He stepped out of the circle and Ishmael stepped in.

"I don't know if Aramus is going to reveal our secrets or not for fear of punishment. But I believe Belial knows something is happening with us and he won't let it be."

Ishmael stepped out of the circle and Abraham took the center.

"Aye, our power to deceive and manipulate is nothing compared to Belial's and we would be smart to consider that. I'm surprised one of us didn't cave while we were inside that steam room, handing him that bunch of bull. He's not stupid and I vote we leave while we can."

Jesseth stepped forward and Abraham took a step back.

"Something is in the air and it is thick. I feel we must end this meeting and go now. We need to flee and stick together. We all have a better chance at survival."

The sound of marching feet quickly approaching and from all directions around the group sent them into a defensive battle formation. They turned their backs to each other so the three men to their right could cover their blind side. Jesseth unsheathed his sword and the group watched the outlying forest fill with the townspeople dressed in battle armor. The townspeople stood shoulder to shoulder and were twenty, maybe thirty people deep, leaving the elite no room to try and flee through the trees or use the foliage as cover.

"Aye, Aramus has forsaken us," Abraham said.

"I will not bow down without being forced to do so," Jesseth said. "And I'll take some with me if this is my final stand,"

"Hold your hand," Sardurvial said.

"But we need to take this opportunity to flee," Ishmael said. "They're still trying to organize and it may be our best and only chance to survive."

"Hold your ground. We aren't cowards!" Jesseth said.

"The law to never watch your chosen victim die is there to keep you from feeling their pain," Sardurvial shouted.

"Shut up, Sardurvial," Aramus said.

"We've all felt their agony and it's unbearable! If you seek what I say, then you will find the truth."

Whap!

Abraham's wings opened and he took to flight. Jesseth, Ishmael and then Sardurvial followed, ascending through the treetops and all went in different directions.

This tactic was used to thin the numbers each one of the elite had to contend with. A swarm of townspeople came up through the treetops in a constant flow, like bees protecting their hive. They all split and gave chase as if Belial anticipated this moment and assigned the townspeople the elite they were responsible for.

Swirling and diving though the air, Sardurvial tried to outmaneuver them, but the faster flyers caught up to him and swatted at him, trying to knock him from the sky. Overwhelmed by the sheer numbers, his wings gave way, tangling and taking him to the ground. Unable to control his descent, he crashed through the trees and slammed into the hard surface cluttered with exposed tree roots. He lay helpless and gasping for breath. The townspeople descended on him and began to stomp him. Without result, he fought back, struggling to fend off and ultimately break free of the overwhelming numbers.

"Stop!" Aramus yelled. "I want him for what he's done to me!"

The townspeople backed away and Aramus took his time to approach Sardurvial.

"I have to walk around with this scar and be reminded of you every time I look in the mirror!" Aramus said. "You deserve this!"

Sardurvial mustered what little fight he had left inside and leapt into the air. He flew through the thick tangle of trees, maneuvering in and out with skill and desperate determination to survive. And when he looked back, he saw no sign of them pursuing him.

Sardurvial and Kathy looked at each other. The tea had gone cold, and the mugs remained nearly full.

"They never caught me again," Sardurvial said. "And on the outskirts of Hell I tried to sort through the pain inside my body and the concern within my mind. I could only hope the others escaped. Things around me happened so fast I didn't have time to think. Without many options I decided I would enter the human world and try to blend there for a while. The move didn't guarantee me anything, but I knew it was my best chance to survive. I figured I could hide among the people.

"The first secure location I stumbled on was the stairwell. I crawled down the steps and gladly lay there until either death called or someone came. You, Kathy, were the first to come along and you seemed pure inside your heart. It appears I made the proper assessment at just a glance."

"But why me?" Kathy said.

"I believe our meeting has been heaven sent, but now Belial has discovered where I am and he's made an attempt to take my life. His attempt wasn't fully carried out because if it was, I would be dead. I think he's prolonging what is coming to make me suffer emotionally for my crimes against him. I accept this, but I will not allow harm to come to you or Jaiden because of my bad decisions. I want you to sleep, Kathy, and I will watch over you while you do so. I will protect you this night and leave you once the day comes. It will be safer for me to travel in the light and it will buy me time to try and find a solution to the mess I've created. I will steal away these memories of everything you've learned to this moment. This is the only way you will be allowed to live and for me to avoid a war because my inability to accept punishment for my wrongdoing. I can get out of this, I just need some more time to think things through."

How ridiculously true Kathy knew this all was. But strangely enough, she could only wonder how she would sleep as Sam suggested. Knowing devils and fallen angels were for real was inconceivable. But knowing they could touch you and bring you harm was something else entirely. It was unreal and elaborately complicated.

"How can you expect me to sleep knowing what you've told me, Sam?" Kathy said.

"I'm going to induce sleep and take away your knowledge of my kind, Kathy. Your belief in godly things will be by faith and faith alone. This is goodbye for us."

Kathy approached Sam, her glassy eyes concentrated into his soft remorseful gaze. The comfort she felt when she was near him was soothing and she liked it and was growing fond of it. Understanding this was what must be, she put that aside. "You've changed for the better Sardurvial and you've helped me experience the feeling of love again. I lost my love one tragic day that was meant for brilliance. Don't take away the love you've allowed me to feel again, that is all I ask."

Kathy kissed Sam's cheek and departed, heading into her bedroom. Before she closed her door for the night, she found she was suddenly and extremely tired, wanting nothing more than to get a good night sleep.

CHAPTER 17

SARDURVIAL, THE WICKED ONE

Sunday, October 16th, 2:43 am

Sam crouched in the corner of the living room. His head was down and his eyes were closed. Unable to rest for even a moment, he remained fully aware and concentrated. He listened for any sound that might reveal the presence of an intruder that sought to harm either himself, Kathy or the young boy.

He opened his eyes and swept the darkness. The house was quiet, and he didn't sense Belial or Aramus.

Drawing a deep breath, he closed his eyes again and listened for foreign sound. The quiet that surrounded the house wouldn't lull him into a false sense of comfort. The circumstances could change in an instant. And in his mind, trouble was going to come before the night was through. That was guaranteed.

Sunday, October 16th, 2:44 am

Inside Kathy's room, an underling of Belial sat in the reading chair at the foot of her bed. Something big was happening and he was excited to be a part of it. He anticipated the moment Belial would unveil its entire splendor and he sensed it was going to be something grand. Careful planning and patience were the components used to ensure its success and he couldn't wait to hear the details.

The underling watched the young woman resting; the blankets that covered her body rose and fell in an uninterrupted rhythm. He hated what he saw and wanted to suck the air out of her lungs and shrink them to the size of a pea. But killing her was not what Belial wanted. Her death would prompt the attention of his enemies and surely the final war would commence. He couldn't imagine being responsible for such a thing so he would do exactly as he was told.

"I will not allow a woman Sardurvial clung to to get away without being punished," Belial had said. "I warned her, but I still have use for her and Sardurvial. I do not want you to cause her physical harm. Do I make myself clear?"

The underling had nodded his head in understanding.

"Good," Belial said with a smile and petted the minion's head. "I want you to enter her mind and show her the one thing that will shake her to her very core. Do you understand my instructions?"

"Yes," the underling had said, eager to please.

"Give her insight into her past so Sardurvial must face her wrath in the morning."

The underling now smiled at Kathy, the memory of his instructions firmly planted into his actions. Concentrating, he opened her mind to his will.

"Sardurvial will come to understand that no matter how far he was to run, he could never escape what he is," the underling whispered. "The time is near that he will beg Belial for his very life."

"You may kiss the bride," the priest said, and Rocco stepped to his new bride and lifted the concealing veil. Kathy smiled widely in nervous anticipation and the thick makeup felt as though it was going to crack around her mouth and lips.

Rocco paused to look into her eyes and there was an intense meaning behind his gaze. It said so much in that moment and Kathy wished she could capture it and keep it forever.

"I love you," Rocco said. "I can't wait to spend the rest of my life with you."

Kathy felt the same way about her new husband and the expression of her love emerged in a trembling wave of joyous tears. Rocco embraced her strongly, passionately, and for the first time they did so as husband and wife. The moment was exquisite. The crowd who had come to share this special day applauded loudly. Husband and wife broke apart and shared a smile with all of their guests. The day was as perfect as any could be.

The wedding party departed. Rocco and Kathy followed them out of the church and hurried through a shower of thrown rice. They scurried into a long stretch white limousine and headed off to nowhere in particular. They would see their friends and family in another three hours when cocktail hour started. For now, it was their time to celebrate alone as husband and wife.

Tyler, drunken and clearly mistaken about his abilities, stumbled out of a bar and headed to his worked up 1978 blue Chevy Nova. Fumbling to open the drivers' side door, he fell into the seat and made several attempts to locate the ignition with his key.

Scraping the steering column before the key awkwardly slid into the slot, Tyler turned the key and cranked the powerful 357 small block.

The passenger door swung open and slammed shut but on a consciousness Tyler couldn't possibly perceive. The alcohol that coursed through his veins didn't play a part in his inability to know about his passenger. The simplicity of his humanity was the cause of that.

Knowing what was going to come if all things went according to plan, Sardurvial made himself as comfortable as he could in the passenger seat and buckled himself in.

"Now," Sardurvial said. "Let me hear the roar of that engine, then take me for a ride. I feel the need for speed."

The voice that commanded the driver remained deaf to his ears, but shouted in decibels to his subconscious mind. The driver obediently obliged and stomped the gas pedal. The engine growled strongly, snapping its teeth and flexing its muscles. Tyler gripped the steering wheel proudly, his white knuckles showing enthusiasm and little restraint. He smiled satisfactorily and shifted the car into reverse and misfortune reared its head. This afternoon was going to end in tragedy for somebody.

Shifting the car into drive, Tyler recklessly steered his car out of the pub parking lot and onto the road. Hitting the gas, he sped forward and left a puff of blue smoke in the air and a track of rubber embossed on the pavement.

"Yeah, come on, show me what this thing has got!" Sardurvial shouted out in pleasure.

Again, Tyler acknowledged the muted command and pushed the pedal to the floor and raced forward. For the first time in his miserable life, he felt liberated and unstoppable. Weaving in and out of traffic, he raced onwards. The light ahead turned yellow and the car was going too fast to stop and Tyler was too drunk to realize he could never hope to make it across the intersection before the light change completed.

"Don't let up Tyler, you can make it!" Sardurvial said and looked out of the passenger window. Slowing motorists and places of business whizzed by, blurred and scribbled by the breakneck speed. He looked forward and saw the light turn red.

Sardurvial shifted his attention to the side window again. He needed to watch the blurred landscape for a while. The law he must obey to never watch his victims die was deeply embedded and controlled his actions. He wasn't quite sure why this rule was there, but it was, and for whatever reason, he didn't have a reason to question it.

Then a thunderous impact of metal slamming into metal at a high rate of speed was deafening. It happened in the middle of the intersection and sent Tyler's Nova into a spin and rolled the car over several times. Tyler died on impact and Sardurvial was violently thrashed about. He continued to ride out the car's flipping without suffering a single scratch.

When the car finally settled, Sardurvial didn't look at the body next to him. He simply unfastened his safety belt and exited the car, leaving the chaos behind without a second thought. Feeling as though it was a job well done, he brushed dirt from his collar and smiled in satisfaction. It was time for him to return home and share this tragedy with Belial and then gladly do whatever was asked of him next.

Kathy pushed herself to her feet and looked down the street. Confusion held her in place and she looked at debris that littered the ground. People approached her from all around and they looked towards her, but not at her. It took her a moment to realize they were looking at something behind her. Everyone seemed horrified and they gasped at what they saw.

She needed to see what it was, but the blue car that sat broken and bent on its rooftop caught her eye. Whatever was there had great meaning to the events that just transpired.

Without a scratch from the impact, she too hurried down the street to have a better look. And as she approached, she realized it wasn't the mangled car that held her curiosity, but rather, it was a person she watched emerge from the wreckage.

"There's a survivor?"

The man stood, brushed off his clothes and looked at Kathy. He was strangely familiar to her although she hadn't ever seen him before.

"Hey, you!" she shouted.

The perplexing stranger turned around and looked at Kathy. His face distorted into a look of disbelief and he turned around and ran away.

"Wait!" Kathy shouted again, but the man ignored her and kept on running.

Disturbed by the idea that someone would flee the scene of such a terrible accident instead of checking on the other people, she took a moment to ponder the events. She tried desperately to put the pieces of the puzzle together.

But no matter how hard she tried to make sense of the events unfolding around her, none of the pieces of the puzzle fit.

People on the street rushed past her.

"I can't believe what I just saw," a young woman said to a man. They might have been boyfriend and girlfriend.

"When I first saw that blue car racing down the street," he said, "I knew it was going too fast to stop. It had to be doing close to a hundred miles an hour when it slammed into the side of that limousine."

"Listen," the girlfriend said. "You can hear someone screaming from the limo."

Kathy listened and could hear a woman's shrill erupting from the wreckage. She ran towards the limo that was nearly split in two, but was stopped by what she saw. Metal was bent in all directions, sharp points angled out like the jaws of a rabid beast. The street was littered with bits of glass and the smell of oil and gasoline was strong.

Rescue workers arrived on scene and began to carve through the wreckage with the Jaws of Life. The loud rattle of the powerful handheld machine held the onlooker's attention.

The machine sputtered to a halt, and the workers toiled tellingly inside the cut vehicle. Tense moments passed slowly.

They pulled a person out. It was a lifeless man, and Kathy recognized him from where she stood.

"Rocco?" she said, and stepped off of the curb and approached. Nobody looked at her or attempted to stop her advancement. She didn't notice their ignorance of her unusually close proximity to the accident nor would she. Rocco's body was bloody, broken and limp and she knew he was already dead.

A stabbing pain in her heart was so powerful that it brought her to her knees. This had happened before and now here she was, being forced to witness it all over again but this time in greater detail. The reoccurring event wasn't any easier to manage this time around.

"Please, not again!" she said, and started to cry.

Yes, again and again until your will is broken!

She often relived the events through dreams, but never had things been so vivid.

Painful howls of anguish came from inside the wreckage and she recognized the voice as being her own. The emotional and physical agony she was in was unforgettable.

Her husband choked his last few breaths of life away with blood dripping from his mouth, eyes and ears, just beyond her reach. She wanted to comfort him but she couldn't reach him. Unable to move, her spine had been broken in three separate places.

"Promise me you will remember me as I was and not as I am before you now," he had said.

"I promise," Kathy said.

He gasped his last breath and she screamed for him to hang on. But he died, and no matter the promise she made to Rocco to uphold his dying request, she learned she couldn't fulfill that agreement.

His face filled with pain and fear haunted her night after night. And as they dragged Rocco out of the metal deathtrap, they just took him further away from her. The look of his fear and pain was emblazed in her brain. And the ache in her back and heart she carried around every day was a constant reminder of the accident and how she lay there broken and bloody, her red dress once white.

Tainted virgin.

How could her fairytale love end in such a heart-rending catastrophe?

Kathy sat up and gasped. Her heart was racing and she was sweating profusely. The content of her dream was irrefutably detailed, providing her with answers to the questions that have haunted her for so long. She now knew the how and why and it only intensified her grief.

Her chest stung and the back of her head throbbed relentlessly. She threw the covers to the side and struggled to stand. The pain in her back returned but the wrenching in her heart overruled it.

Short of breath and making her way to the bath-room, she ran water and splashed it on her face.

"No!" she shouted, and dropped to her knees and howled out in bitter anguish.

She hated the answers she'd been given. How could she have been such a fool to think someone like him could change and find purity? She could never forgive him for ruining her life!

CHAPTER 18

DECEIT AND MURDER

Sunday, October 16th, 9:22 am

Sam followed Kathy to the bathroom, his presence undetected. He planned to keep himself hidden from her eyes and take a moment to watch her before he set off in search of Jesseth, Ishmael and Abraham. He could only hope they were as lucky as he'd been and they were able to escape the townspeople sent to kill them.

Where should he begin his search?

He would have enough time to decide after he took his leave. For now, he was going to take a moment to give a bittersweet farewell to a wonderful person who taught him much. He felt his heart sink; he would miss her terribly. He'd begun to care for her but it was time for him to move on. The sun had risen and a new day had come, and for Sardurvial it was bright and promising but there was no illusion that it would be without challenge.

Kathy splashed her face with water and began to sob. Sam stepped forward, concern delaying his leave.

Kathy fell to her knees and began to wail.

Sam held his ground and watched her, his heart breaking. Indecisively he stepped forward to embrace her. He paused again, realizing he could no longer do such a thing. He remembered before she lay down for the night, he'd taken all memory of his kind out of her mind. That was when he said his final goodbye. He kept her safe until morning like he promised and now he needed to move on to ensure her safety.

"I'm sorry, Kathy. I don't know what has pulled you from your sleep and what has you so upset, but this one you'll have to face on your own. You're strong and I know you will get you through it."

He turned and began to walk away.

Unbeknownst to Sam's heightened awareness, Kathy stood and looked at him. Unabashed hatred filled her face and her eyes were red and wide with rage. She stared at him hard, her look burning a hole into his back, her mind thinking only one thing: the bastard!

"Sardurvial!" she growled, her voice possessed by the betrayal she felt crushing her heart.

Sam stopped, his doubt hesitating him. Did he just hear Kathy summoning him? "Impossible," his mind argued, knowing how careful he was when he wiped all memory of his kind from her mind. He should be invisible to her eyes as well as deaf to her ears. He turned to see, slow and hesitant in his investigation. Before him she stood, her eyes focused on him, ablaze with abhorrence.

"It was you!" she said with scorn. "You encouraged that kid to drink in the bar and get in his car! You were the one who influenced him to drive drunk and speed through the intersection! You're the one responsible for the accident that killed my Rocco!"

Sam stammered at the accusation. He knew exactly what Kathy was talking about. Memories of that day sped through his mind: the bar, the revved up car, the suggestion to take a spin and the horrible sound of the collision. And then there was the vivid memory of him walking away from the scene of the accident without care and the woman who noticed him. How come he didn't remember that until now?

"You killed my husband!" Kathy growled, and stepped forward and slapped Sam. "You broke my damn back!"

Sam's head rattled. He looked at her and saw the hatred burning within her eyes. Insatiable. He didn't blame her, though. He backed away and searched for reason. There was none. Only guilt and shame of what he once was and for the things he'd done in the name of some war that no longer made any sense to him.

"I'm . . . I'm sorry," he muttered and hung his head.

"Sorry?" Kathy said, the hate tangible. She lunged forward and slapped his face again.

Sam's head rocked and his ear buzzed from the force of the blow. He refused to defend himself to her fury. He ruined her life and he could never forgive himself for that. "I cannot expect you to understand that Belial had foreseen this moment and planned it to happen all along," Sam said, unsure exactly how this was all supposed to play out.

Kathy's eyes constricted and the hate that filled her soul rolled off the end of her tongue in a fiery fit of rage. "And I cannot hope to make you understand what hell you've made of my life! To think someone like you, a destroyer of hopes and dreams, could show me how to love again. Get out of my house and never return here again, you bastard! I hate you for what you've done to me and my family!"

Sam remained still, not wanting to obey her command. If he could only calm her so he could explain the reasons why, he knew he might gain her forgiveness.

"I told you I want you to leave. Now get out of here you bastard!" she shouted and pushed him.

Sam turned and headed towards the door. He felt her hate and he didn't want to be around it. It scared him a little, made him uncomfortable. If only she would understand that his life was a living hell too. Knowing the things he had done were hard to live with and inescapable.

But she didn't do that to him, did she?

The thought was like a knife that was slowly sinking into his skin, entering his heart. He did that to her, and he alone. He pushed the guilt aside and slid the chain away. Unlocking the deadbolt and grabbing the knob, he twisted it. Pausing, he turned and faced Kathy. "For what little comfort it can provide you with, Kathy, I am sorry. I cannot undo all the wrongs I've done. There aren't enough lifetimes left for me to make that up. I can only better myself from this day forward by doing what's right. If my leaving is what's right for you—"

"Get out!"

He pulled the door open and Sam jumped back in surprise. Megan stood in the threshold of the doorway, her head down and her hair draped in front of her face. Her jacket was torn and dangled off her shoulders and she was sobbing.

"Megan?" Sam said, sensing something wasn't right and it was something much deeper than the surface wounds. He searched for what it was.

"Megan?" Kathy said, her anger turned to concern and she approached the door.

Sam moved aside and allowed Kathy enough room to stand in front of her sister. He continued to study Megan in search of what stirred beneath the surface. Whatever it was hid deep and didn't want to be discovered.

Kathy bent at her knees and pushed her sister's hair to the side. "I don't want to touch you for fear of hurting you. What hurts?"

"Everything," Megan said.

Dried blood was crusted to her nostrils and caked around her lips. Her left eye was swollen shut and a purplish knot decorated her cheekbone. Her right eye wandered aimlessly and she shook.

Kathy led Megan into the house and sat her down on the couch.

Sam closed the door and locked it, still searching for what he sensed. Hurrying to the bathroom, he fetched a warm washcloth for Kathy and then watched in wait while she helped her sister. Kathy took the wet cloth and crouched next to her sister and began to clean her face with gentle dabs.

"You need to speak to me Megan and tell me what hurts."

Sam remembered when Kathy did that for him, and he couldn't help but acknowledge the intense pain he suddenly noticed wrenching his heart. He was reminded of what he was asked to do two years ago. If only he would've known. He'd wrought so much havoc and slaughtered on Belial's behalf using blind obedience. And this pained him more than anything. How could he ever face the burden of everything he's ever done and make it right?

"What happened, Megan? Who did this to you?" Kathy said.

"I don't know what to say," Megan said.

"Whatever it is, it's okay. I'll help you through it."

Megan looked up from her lap and her dampened hair was clingy and knotted. It shielded her face like a grass straw swathe. Kathy brushed her hair to the side and saw her sister was crying silently.

Tears streaked her face and dripped from her quivering chin. "I'm so sorry," Megan said. "I lied to you, Kathy."

Megan wailed and buried her face in her hands.

"How did you lie to me Megan?"

"You're going to hate me. I don't want to say it."

"I'm not going to hate you. I never could. You're my sister and I love you."

"You won't after this," Megan said. "You're going to think I'm a monster."

Kathy rubbed Megan's back and mustered a soft sympathetic tone. "Tell me what happened."

Megan fought the tears away, threw her head back and looked into her sister's eyes. "I never went out with my friends last night and I never had plans to go out with them. I really had plans to go and meet up with Ted."

"Why would you do that?"

"Because I'm a fool, that's why."

"He did this to you, didn't he?"

Megan wiped her eyes. "I know what I did last night was stupid and wrong."

Kathy folded her arms.

"Ted told me he's been going for help and that he'd changed. He said he didn't feel angry anymore and that he quit drinking. For Jaiden Michael's sake I wanted to believe him and work things out. I really did. I wanted more than anything to have my family back together again."

"Oh Megan . . ."

"When I met him, he seemed like he was back to the same person I first fell in love with. I was happy again. I mean truly happy. We had dinner together, and afterwards he invited me back to his place and I declined. He told me the invitation was innocent, that we needed to discuss Jaiden's needs and get along as friends. I believed he was being sincere and I decided to go. But at his house he came onto me and I turned him down. He got really mad and started beating me. Years ago I learned not to try and resist his advances when he got physical, so I gave into him and let him have his way. When he fell asleep, I left. I've been walking around for hours, trying to figure out what I should do."

"We've got to go call the police. Fill out a report and have him arrested," Kathy said and stood. "You can't shower or anything."

Megan shook her head and remained seated. "No, Kathy, I don't want to go to the police. I'm embarrassed by what I've done and I just want it to go away."

"It's not going to just disappear. You have to do something," Kathy said, her voice growing loud with frustration. "You can't let him get away with what he's done!"

"I have to," Megan said, shamefully settling, her will beaten. "I don't want to have to explain why I went to his house willingly when I had an order of protection against him. What will they think and what will they say about me? I can't put myself through that. I have Jaiden to think about."

"Mom?" Jaiden said from the hallway. He dug at his eyes with the heels of his hands.

Megan looked away. "Go back into the bedroom, Jaiden, Mommy will be there in a minute. I'm having a talk with your Aunt Kathy."

"What's wrong, Mommy?" Jaiden said, his voice filled with fright.

Kathy got up and hurried over to Jaiden. "Give me a minute with him," she said, and ushered Jaiden back to the bedroom. She took him inside and closed the door.

Megan slowly raised her head, pushed her hair away from her face and wiped her eyes. She smiled warmly, and with the voice of Belial, she said, "You sensed me but couldn't finger it. You're losing your touch."

The moment of realization slammed into Sardurvial like Tyler's Nova into the side of the limo. The insight nearly sent him down. The only thing that kept him vertical was the disbelief Belial could actually be inside Megan's body.

Megan stood and swayed confidently in Sardurvial's apprehension. "That's right, Sardurvial," she said, her voice deep and her smile never dwindling. "You didn't think I would allow you to get away with what you've done, did you? That story I told Kathy was great, wasn't it? Big bad Teddy beat me up!" Megan snickered and danced about, Belial controlling all functions of the body effortlessly.

"Obviously not a completely true story, but a good believable one unlike that line of crap you and the others tried to give me about stealing horses and riding them around. What kind of fool do you think I am? I heard your entire story, Sardurvial. I was within the forest watching you all. The trees provided me with shadows I used to hide in. I moved around in them gracefully, listening to the echoes of the wind carrying your voices to me. The trees of this world serve me as everything else does. Look at this . . ."

Megan lifted up her shirt and on her abdomen there was several puncture wounds that had been poorly cleaned and dressed. She pulled down her shirt. "Don't draw any conclusions as to what happened here, Sardurvial. Hear my story first. I'm sure you'll find it's quite creative and to your liking.

"Do you remember the way you followed Lenny around and subliminally corrupted him? You know, get real close to his ear and whisper some evil suggestions here and there. This is the way you can get Redhead, blah, blah, blah. I knew full well Megan was going to see that abusive bastard Ted last night. I was there, within her house when she first made the plans. I planned to use the moment to my advantage. When the time came, I had him kill her. He stabbed her to death after she willingly gave him sex. It was satisfyingly messy and loud."

Belial paused and pondered deeply. He smiled in satisfaction and shared his thoughts. "They were having sex and I whispered something in Ted's ear. What was it? Oh, yes, I remember now." Belial changed his voice to match Megan's. "I'm screwing your friend and you're too stupid to realize this. That's why I split up with you and created such a distance between us. You're only getting it now because I feel sorry for you."

Belial changed his voice back to his own.

"You've used that approach, haven't you, Sardurvial? It works wonders, I know. I've seen the affects of what our influence can cause. Such power! I decided to step inside Megan's body and take full control of it once her soul left the shell. Though I find it to be a bit stuffy in here, I do find it's serving its purpose well."

Sam grabbed the wall to keep himself from falling.

"Jesseth has already been taken care of," Belial said. "Ishmael and Abraham will be dealt with accordingly. I can assure you that I have plans for them. Creative and tormenting, just like what I've planned for you. Oh, and about the Kathy woman knowing the sick details behind her wedding day accident? I felt she needed to know what misery you've composed for her life. Why should you be looked upon as a knight in shining armor when you're nothing but an Angel who has chosen to walk away from God's good grace? You can never escape the hell you've created for yourself, Sardurvial. You know an Angel can never return to Heaven once he falls. To be in God's presence and reject it for hope I could offer something better may not have been the wisest decision. What I failed to mention was that my agenda was actually more than I was willing to say. It included my overthrowing God and taking His throne to lead in Heaven. You see, I can prove He is imperfect and I can do better. And now I come to find after I offer you a chance at greatness, you've decided not to accept it and walk out on me? Where do you think you can go? Amongst the human cattle I've made you hate?"

Belial tittered.

Sam looked towards the spare bedroom and saw Kathy emerging from it. Frenetically he looked back at Megan, and thankfully, he saw she was returning to the couch. Attempting to appear composed. Sam stood but remained tense as he watched Kathy settle unknowingly next to her sister that was no longer what she once was: a precious caring soul, a mother of a beautiful young boy that would sacrifice anything for the safety of her son and sister. Now she was just an empty shell housing the wickedest and most calculating entity this world had ever seen.

"Jaiden's okay," Kathy said. "He understands we're having an adult discussion that he cannot hear." Kathy's hands shook and she was fidgety. She neatened Megan's hair best she could.

Megan smiled. "Thank you for your help, Kathy." Her smile disappeared and she became withdrawn.

"Talk to me Megan," Kathy said.

"There is something else I have to tell you."

Kathy turned askew, taking her sister's hands into her own. Compassion seeped from Kathy's stare.

"I lied to you before and you need to know the truth. I didn't leave his house when he fell asleep. I stood over him, listening to him snore as if he didn't care at all about what he did to me. So I stuck a knife in his belly. My hate for him and the lies he's convinced me as being truth possessed me. I lifted up the knife and brought it down and he awoke. His eyes went wide as if he was disbelieving what was happening to him. He gurgled as he tried to plead for his life. The only thing I could think of was being done with him forever. I couldn't stop my attack until I knew for sure he was dead. It was terrible, Kathy. I can't stop thinking about it! Blood was everywhere and I can still see his face looking at me, judging me for what I'd done!"

Kathy remained completely still, unable to form an expression or even a word.

Megan cried hysterically.

Sardurvial detested Belial's games and wished desperately to put an end to it. But for fear of Kathy and Jaiden's safety he knew he couldn't act. All he could do was wait and see what Belial had planned to bring him suffering.

"I'm sorry, I shouldn't have come here and put this all on you. I should go, Kathy," Megan said and stood.

Kathy moved to her feet, the shock of the moment continued to hold her tongue.

"Please, watch over Jaiden for me," Megan said and sprinted to the door. She fumbled to unlock it, but managed and ran out. She pulled the door closed behind her, the door slammed, rattling the windows in their frames.

Kathy was yanked from her trance, ran to the door and yanked it open. "Megan, wait!"

But her cry came too late.

Megan threw herself forward and tumbled down the steps, her body bending in ways it wasn't designed to move. Bones broke, poorly sealed wounds tore open, and the body settled twisted and devoid of life on the bottom step.

Kathy ran from her apartment, Sardurvial followed close behind, and descended the steps quickly, falling down and skipping steps on their way. Pausing on the landing, Kathy stood over her sister and quivered.

"No!" she screamed and fell to her knees, hovering over her sister's broken body.

Sardurvial went to Kathy and tried to comfort her. She thwarted him with a blow. "Look at what you've caused you bastard!"

Sardurvial knew what Kathy said was true. His decisions caused her this great pain and there was nothing he could do to change what was. But there was something he could do and the thought frightened him. He could turn himself in to Belial. Make an even exchange. His life for mercy on the kind hearted woman who continued to suffer because of him.

Sardurvial said nothing. He simply turned away and headed outside. Pausing to sniff the chilly night air, he fought to hold back the growing storm of emotion welling in his chest. He believed for the first time he could not win this fight. He was no match for Belial and he was foolish for having thought he was. He was lucky he survived one night.

One lousy night.

Playing the fool seemed to be his part.

Feeling the torment within swelling, moving up his throat, Sardurvial descended the steps and hid in the abandoned stairwell he discovered the night he escaped Hell. While there, he attempted to cry some of the ache away.

CHAPTER 19

INFLUENCE

Sunday, October 16th, 11:43 pm

Kathy was lying in bed with her eyes closed and the lights off. Jaiden Michael was sitting on the foot of the bed distantly quiet, watching his aunt. Kathy was lost in her own thoughts but for reasons that were far different than Jaiden's. For her, the death of her sister and the horrific details she relayed to the police about the previous night loomed within her psyche. It was unthinkable to imagine her sister was pushed so far that she would kill the father of her own child and then herself. Searching for understanding had given her a tremendous headache that was beyond aggravating. It was throbbing and unrelenting and powerful enough to push her into silence. All hope of happiness in her life was gone forever. The death of her husband drained the love from her heart, and the death of her sister sucked the life out of her soul. In this troubled moment she believed if it wasn't for Jaiden she would . . .

Kathy shook her head in an attempt to dislodge that train of thought. It was against her beliefs to do something like that. It was a coward's way out and she was anything but a coward. Her thought shifted to the recent dealings with the police. It was painful, but she told them everything her sister had said word for word. But Kathy never mentioned anything about the man named Sardurvial. Things surrounding his presence and sudden disappearance would only complicate things more than they already were. The police investigated and confirmed that Ted, Megan's husband, was found dead and his wounds were consistent with the story Kathy recited. Kathy would have to live with the cold distant stare she saw in her sister's eyes when she lay askew at the bottom of the steps. Lonely, in pain, and shameful in her misery, it was the same look her husband had inside the twisted wreckage of the limousine.

The pain she felt had a strong pull from long taut fingers that wished to pull her into eternal despair. Refocusing, she knew she had to stay beyond its reach. She now had someone else she needed to look after, someone else she needed to put before her own feelings. The well-being of a child depended on her ability to adapt and overcome these tragedies.

As for Jaiden Michael, if he were in charge of his own emotions he would wail out in anguish for the loss of his parents. He was old enough to know what death meant and the finality of it. He was faced with death many times in his room alone at night—all those beasts looking to drag him into the abyss within his closet. The loss of his parents was a devastating blow, but he would survive and learn to cope. He was a strong boy and for the moment, someone *within* him was making sure he remained sheltered from that heart wrenching pain that would drag him into despair. But, when the time finally came when that "someone" lurking *within* could no longer remain and protect him from what was anxiously awaiting his vulnerability, it would be up to his Aunt Kathy to love and nurture the boy into a healthy young man.

The unseen presence contemplated this notion and smiled confidently. Kathy was strong and more than able to face whatever fate may have laid out for her. She would survive. She was strong, a foundation built tough enough for two. She'd been through hell once and she came out on top and that was more than the presence could say for himself. If only he were a little like her.

Jaiden slid off the bed and walked around the bedside and looked down on his aunt. Though the lingering darkness and the web of blankets concealed the expression she held, Jaiden Michael knew his aunt was distraught; he could feel her sadness from where he stood. It was a thwarting feeling, the sadness was, and it was beyond his understanding. But somehow he understood its meaning completely; it was a depressing feeling that could only be extinguished by acts of love.

The presence within was helping him solve these puzzles and all *he* wanted was for his aunt to cry out and not stop doing so until all her pain was gone or exhaustion overtook her and pushed her into a deep undisturbed sleep. Until that time came he silently decided he was going to do anything he could to provide her with the comfort and love she needed. Though Jaiden didn't make the decision on his own accord, he would never know it. His inability to detect the unknown presence within was beyond human comprehension. And what he and his aunt were going through could never be understood, whether that was a simple child or a brilliant adult.

"Aunt Kathy?" Jaiden said in a whisper, his tone kept low for the sake of compassion.

She rolled to her side, facing him; penetrating light that beamed through the pulled shades showed her face. Her eyes were heavy and glassy and her voice was rough when she spoke. "Yes, sweetie?"

Jaiden stood erect and swallowed hard. He didn't like what he saw and for a fleeting moment he could feel her sorrow. It was consuming like the break of a persistent tide. The presence within quickly masked such feelings and provided Jaiden with strength and guidance to help both he and his aunt through such troubled times. "Are you okay?" Jaiden asked, genuinely concerned. "Can I get you something from the kitchen? You haven't had anything to eat all day."

Kathy smiled. "A glass of warm milk and some toast would be great, Jaiden."

"Okay, I'll be right back." Jaiden smiled outwardly and quickly turned away and scurried out of the room.

Kathy shared the moment of simple pleasure without pain in either her heart or lower back and she watched Jaiden exit the room. With a deep sigh, she sank into the bed.

"I'm sorry for thinking the way I did," Kathy whispered into the still room. "He's a great boy and I will never leave him, Megan." She heard the flat tone of her promise bounce duly off the walls. The quiet that followed and swallowed everything in the room added no relief; it only brought back the pain she'd momentarily escaped. Then as sudden as the silence settled, it was interrupted by something nameless. At its sound, Kathy shivered and sat up abruptly. Hugging her blankets for the sake of security, she listened to the sounds of the room intently, swearing she heard a response to her promise. It said, "I know you will."

CHAPTER 20

THE PAST, FUTURE AND PRESENT

Sunday, October 16th, 10:24 am

Sardurvial used his unearthly abilities to shield his presence from any human that might come upon him while he lay in the stairwell. Though overwhelmed and afraid of what Belial might do next, he took a moment to feel his surroundings out. A moment of contentment shielded him; all was quiet. He acknowledged the comfort the stairwell had provided him. Its blackened cavity had given him enough protection to stay the night after the attack, and now, returning for that same result; he remained undetected. He welcomed the cold brick walls and cement slab as his home, his new heaven. It was a place of refuge where he would be able to escape the misery and violence of this world and the next.

Listening to the commotion begin to form above as the police arrived at the tragedy spread about the apartment house lobby, Sardurvial placed his head down and tried to figure a plan. He knew he was going to have to face Belial, but how was he going to do it without all the townspeople getting to him first? Some he would be able to slip by undetected, but most were as powerful as he was and have heightened senses that were almost impossible to avoid. Though most were not as skilled in the art of combat as he, he did understand he would be able to kill some, but he was sure he'd be overwhelmed within moments since their numbers were great.

There was no plan good enough to be able to trap Belial. He was far too powerful and had way too many who believed in him and that would willingly die for him without a second thought. With such thoughts spinning about his head, Sardurvial pondered the vivid memory of two that dissented not so long ago. It was a story the elite touched on while they made their way to the clearance in the forest but Abraham didn't want to talk about it. He realized it was that moment that was responsible for changing him.

He and the others were sitting in the tavern enjoying a beer and speaking about that day's events that were, as usual, eventful and exciting. He could remember the atmosphere of the tavern being louder than usual. After all, it was a night to celebrate. The construction of their hell had been recently completed and several thousand more angels fell from the sky throughout the course of the day. When questioned it was learned that they too had distrusted God and confronted Him about their concerns. Their sentence was the same as the first group that fell long before them: eternity on earth, forever alienated from God's grace. Belial took them in with open arms. He joyously celebrated how much his army grew that day, and knowing chaos still filled the Heavens couldn't raise his spirits any higher.

Sardurvial wondered if the newly fallen thought going down in the world below was some sort of revelry.

The fools.

If they only knew the staggering number behind those that were silently miserable because of their separation from God. Those that hated what they'd become and wished they could undo it, but instead they had to convince themselves that they were right. That being separated from God's perfect love wasn't painful.

For the moment Sardurvial could only dream of exchanging places with one that would be foolish enough to not realize what they had and what they would be missing. It was a constant longing that was impossible to fulfill.

His thoughts shifted to when he and the other members of the elite were the first to welcome the newly fallen into their society. They sat them down in the tavern to have one drink with them. The elite socializing with the "regular" townspeople was expected to be kept to a minimal by a strict request from Belial. He always made it his business to express how they were "better" than the others, and therefore, they needed to act it. Sardurvial and the others upheld that image well; many feared them.

After they entertained the new group, the elite moved to their own table they'd long ago claimed as their own and began conversing about the new arrivals. No sooner did a nervous Angel who pushed his way through the thick crowd bump into the table the elite occupied and spilt their beer. Sardurvial looked at him with a tightened expression, showing the nameless angel what he'd done was a foolish mistake.

"Sorry," the nameless angel panted. He was sweating and had a concerned look about him. The elite remained quiet to hear why he'd been sent to them.

"Belial needs to see you," he said. "He said your presence before him is an urgent matter, but he wishes you not to draw attention to yourselves."

The elite exchanged glances and stood. As Abraham departed with his comrades, he said to the nameless angel, "Aye, unlike what you've done coming here to relay this message to us, chap?"

The nameless angel looked over his shoulder and saw the patrons of the tavern were staring in their direction. "Sorry, sire. Belial told me to move with haste."

When the elite arrived in the steam room, Belial was on his raft shuffling through pages lined with gold that he guarded from their eyes. Beside the steaming hot pool, the unit gathered. While they waited, Belial took his time in going through the papers. When he was done, he placed them on his lap and paddled the raft before his men and appraised them.

"There is something I must ask of you all," Belial said. "Again, what I speak of can never be spoken from your lips or thought of in a dream. It has come to my attention that two from our community have desired to break my rule to never watch a victim die. They have done so and now find that they cannot face what they've found. Do what you must to return them here, alive. Under no circumstance are you to ask them questions about what I tell you or allow them to share such. I do not want my elite tainted. Are my orders clear?"

In unison the elite nodded in full understanding.

"Good," Belial said, and he began to paddle away from them. "They've just entered the southern region of the unexplored forest. You'll find them there. Hurry along."

The elite quickly disbursed. They began their journey to the southern forest region by air. Along the way, the group spoke to one another freely about their mission.

"This is the third time in recent weeks we're searching out some of our own for the same bloody reason," Abraham said.

Aramus nodded in agreement, his wings displacing the wind with grace and authority. "And with the same instructions each time. I wonder what it is they saw that has them running?"

Jesseth shook his head in worry and he checked behind himself. "No, Aramus," Jesseth said. "Don't think such things, it will only find you trouble."

"I agree," said Sardurvial as he flew in close and tightened their formation. "It seems to me Belial has eyes and ears all about. We must be careful with what we say and do. We are his most trusted, and I'm led to believe his most watched. He doesn't want to be made the fool. You never know, he may be testing our ability to follow his instructions and testing our loyalty. These two may not have done anything and they could be reporting back to Belial."

"Aye," Abraham said. "Good point, chap, and I agree. Especially being that I haven't heard anything about the others we brought back earlier in the week."

"I've heard they'd been executed," Ishmael said. "That seems to be the word around town."

"The word around town?" Aramus said. "How could that be if we're the only ones to know about these missions?"

Ishmael shrugged. "I'm only saying what I heard."

"Belial," Sardurvial said. "He did it to scare those that might be tempted to break his rule. I fear if the mission we're on now is a legit dissention, then these two will be facing terrible punishment. But that isn't our concern. The betterment of our community is. And those who will disrupt our land will be brought to Belial to face punishment for what they've done."

"Aye," said Abraham in agreement.

"Enough talk for now," Sardurvial said and dipped away from the tight formation he'd been flying in. "We are near now and we must concentrate on our duties. Ishmael, Jesseth and Abraham, you three stay in the air like last time. Aramus and I will flush the two vermin out of the forest for you."

Sardurvial and Aramus dove together, dropping into the dense forest. Remaining silent to survey the area, the two slowly advanced, paused every thirty paces and listened again until they heard the voices of the escapees. Listening to their conversation to get a better understanding of their mood, Sardurvial and Aramus stealthily closed in.

"I must rest, I tell you. My feet are killing me," one escapee said to the other.

The other shook his head in disagreement. "We can't ever do that again! I'm telling you Belial knows about what we've done and he's going to send someone after us. Telling us to take the day for ourselves is something he only does for his elite. He just has to know, I can feel it!"

"Belial knows all," Sardurvial said.

The two dissenters paused in fear. They dropped their bags and began to run. Sardurvial and Aramus gave chase, quickly catching up to them. In a desperate attempt to escape capture, the two dissenters leapt into the air and took to flight. Crashing through the interlocked treetops, Sardurvial and Aramus halted their pursuit and looked at one another in successful appreciation.

"We'll give the boys above the chance to get in on some of the action," Sardurvial said. Aramus nodded in agreement. After waiting a few moments, they took to flight, ascending through the path torn through the trees by the fleeing dissenters.

Jesseth maintained control over the dissenters with the tip of his sword bouncing back and forth between the two of them. He was threatening to slash their throats at any unexpected move.

As Sardurvial and Aramus approached, one was pleading with Abraham. He was trying to explain why he was running. Aramus went before him and placed his pointer finger to his lips. He made a hushing sound and the Angel immediately calmed and quieted.

"We're not interested in what you have to say," Sardurvial said. "So don't waste your breath. You've broken the law."

His focus returned to the present, and he realized their demanded silence was worse than any explanation they might have given for running. It was what piqued his curiosity and whether he wanted to admit it at the time or not, he did want to hear what they had to say. And the only thing that kept him from saying so was his fear of Belial.

His focus returned to the past again and he remembered escorting the two escapees back to Belial where he waited in the steam room. Belial, occupying the raft, smiled proudly at the sight of his elite and plunged himself into the steaming water without reaction. He treaded the water to the staircase and watched the two escapees with disdain. When he settled before them, he shook his head in displeasure.

"You two baffle me," Belial said, and the two captives trembled. "I told you that I know everything. Did you not believe me, or did you take my momentary silence of the matter as pure ignorance? I've made plans for you and any that dare to make a decision such as you have."

Belial turned to his elite.

"Gentlemen. Escort these infidels outside. There is a lesson to be learned here today."

Truly unknowing the meaning behind Belial's last statement, the elite marched the two prisoners outside. To their surprise, the townspeople were gathered around. All were quiet and their eyes showing befuddled anticipation.

What had Belial planned?

Sardurvial was sure no one knew other than Belial himself and this made him uneasy.

Belial soon emerged, a blank look about his face. He stood before his people in silent contemplation. Then he addressed them with authority. "It seems as though discipline is a continuing problem for some of the members of our society. Three times in recent weeks I've had to send the elite out to deal with the same thing. I call them dissenters. Why do we have them?" Belial scoped the crowd with widened eyes. "The answer is simple: because they did not adhere to the law and constant warnings not to break them. We are not to be tempted by anything! *We* are the tempters of this world!"

Belial turned to his elite.

"Put them on their hands and knees and strip them of their clothing."

The elite acted quickly. Watching until the dissenters were subdued in the position he wanted them in, Belial turned back to the crowd.

"I feel the pain of my people," Belial said, and turned to Jesseth and held his hand out. "Give me your sword!"

Jesseth unsheathed his sword and handed it over to Belial, handle first. Belial held the sword up high, displaying its craftsmanship to the crowd. "Dissenters will no longer be tolerated! It affects our society in many ways. Ways that we cannot afford to face. United we stand. Divided we fall!"

The elite continued to hold the squirming escapees down. Belial positioned himself beside one of the dissenters and he grabbed hold his wing. The prisoner tried to fight Belial's grasp, but Belial outstretched the wing fully and cut it off, leaving a stump. The dissenter screamed out in agony and Belial responded with a grunt of his own. Trying to stay strong in front of his people, Belial clipped the other wing and did the same to the second dissenter. He panted heavily and staggered as he walked, weakened by the shared trauma.

"I will find no mercy in my heart for one that dissents ever again!" Belial ordered his elite to stand the prisoners up and position them stomach to back. They did, and Belial plunged the sword into their bellies, impaling them both. Belial gurgled along with them and spat blood as they died. Throwing the sword to the ground, Belial made his way inside. The townspeople stood in silence, looking at the devastation Belial left behind.

Sardurvial's thoughts returned to the present. He understood he had become those men he held to the ground and he and the other three were the first to dissent since this incident. He knew he must wait until Belial came again and stood his ground when that time came or that same fate would be his. The thought frightened him, but he knew it was his only option. When he woke, he planned to move as far away from Kathy and Jaiden as he possibly could. His existence caused them enough pain.

Sardurvial rested his head on his forearms and he closed his eyes. Leaving Hell and surviving was something he could make work. It required little detail. For one, fast movement that was constant and quiet was a necessity. Another important factor included interacting with as few people as possible and shielding his thoughts at all times. Satisfied with the small accomplishment of having something planned beyond the now, Sardurvial sighed with relief and hope, believing he could do that.

A total state of relaxation consumed him and he quickly descended into sleep. Each moment that passed, he fell deeper and deeper, allowing himself to become more and more vulnerable. A penetrating light infiltrated his tranquil state and began to play out visions from a not too distant future.

Sardurvial hovered outside a window some twenty feet above ground level and was looking inside a darkened room. What he could make out was a bed, dresser and reading chair. It was all so familiar to him, yet so foreign. And for the moment he was unsure what he was doing there.

Continuing to peer inside the room, he searched closely, looking for his purpose. The reading chair at the foot of the bed was empty. The bed itself had a mound of blankets on it, twisted in such a heap it seemed impossible for anyone to comfortably remain underneath or even be able to draw breath through its mass.

Sardurvial continued to hover and inspect the room, everything looked so familiar but the clues couldn't be further away. The bedroom door swung open and a young boy holding a food tray stepped inside the room and approached the side of the bed. Light pouring through the doorway cast the boy's shadow across the bed and it stretched up the wall, covering the window Sardurvial was peering through.

Sardurvial could see someone beneath the covers began to stir. He watched the shifting mound of covers with anticipation. Swinging to the left, he was attempting to see better, but the boy's shadow continued to block his view.

The boy placed the bed tray across the person who was now sitting up in bed. He then retreated to the foot of the bed where he settled.

Sardurvial could see the person lying in bed was a woman; the bushy hair and slim build told him that. He knew her, but from where he wasn't exactly sure. Things were foggy. He pressed his ear against the window in hopes of recognizing her voice.

"Thank you, Jaiden," the woman said. Sardurvial pulled his ear away from the glass, suddenly realizing who the woman was and what he'd done to her. Pain flooded his heart in an overpowering rush and he began to drift downwards. How could he ever forget her and the anguish he'd caused her?

Upon touching the ground, Sardurvial settled on his heels and looked up at the window. He couldn't help but relate the room Kathy was in to a cage where a suffering animal had been locked away to bear pain it could never understand or hope to overcome. God, he wished he could make everything normal again, and not only for himself, but for Kathy and the boy as well. But that was an unrealistic craving. To undo what he'd done would unravel what went before. And the past, unlike the lives of the people, was something he never had the power to manipulate. Was that saying the same rule applied for the future? No, that was predestining living and why would God grant freewill if everything anyone ever did were already set in stone? It made no sense. Freewill was freewill. A decision is what changed lives and the paths people were to walk on. Now, Sardurvial could only wonder if the trials and tribulations were something he had to endure because of something larger than his own understanding. He couldn't help but think that was so.

He knew he was supposed to move on so he could lure Belial away from Kathy's home but he felt something wasn't right. It was a bad feeling that was surrounding the apartment building, and knowing that, he couldn't leave her. He had to look her over one last time to be sure she was all right. To verify the feeling he was experiencing was nothing more than a way to escape the guilt that would punish him persistently if he didn't. Sardurvial ascended to the window and began his quiet observation of the room Kathy and Jaiden occupied.

Kathy was sitting up with her back resting on the headboard. She placed an empty cup on the breakfast tray before her and said something to Jaiden seated at the foot of the bed. Sardurvial was unable to decipher the words being communicated between the two. He watched the boy laugh and stand from the foot of the bed and take the tray off of his aunt's lap. He placed it on the night table beside the bed and he fiddled with the objects on the tray.

Jaiden turned to his aunt and said something, his expression hard. Sardurvial watched Kathy's expression fail. She was suddenly disturbed, angered even. The boy began to shout, his fury obvious through his narrowed gaze and clenched fists. Kathy retaliated by yelling back and shifting to her side, turning her back to her nephew.

Sardurvial couldn't help but notice how out of context this was for the two of them. Kathy was normally fun loving and easy going, and Jaiden was quiet and respectful. Maybe, he thought, it was the stress of the past few days. Tomorrow when they woke, things would be better.

But suddenly Jaiden turned around and retrieved a knife from the breakfast tray. Without hesitation he thrust the knife into his aunt's back and withdrew it. He sunk it in her again and again, his eyes like a demon possessed.

Kathy's taut hands clawed the air and her eyes widened as if she was watching her soul depart; disbelief consumed her, the pain paralyzed her. Now who would care for her nephew?

Jaiden dropped the bloody knife and Sardurvial heard it clunk on the wooden floor. Like the moment in the forest with Lenny and Redhead, he was unable to move. Dissenting against Belial caused this and every tragedy before it to unfold. If he'd only kept his mouth shut inside the forest.

Jaiden stepped away from the bed, his mouth opened wide, stretching beyond its natural elasticity. The skin tore back to his ears, and his young hands reached up and helped peel the skin back, making room for something significant beneath to emerge. Sardurvial could only watch in horror. Somehow he'd forgotten about some of the players involved, and he could only wonder how he could've been so careless not to think they were near.

The boy's skin was peeled down like a bodysuit and Aramus stepped out of it. Covered with blood and gore, he looked at Sardurvial. He smiled long and hard, and then licked the crevice in his lip and casually skipped away.

Dread consumed Sardurvial. To harm a human can mean only one thing: Belial must be ready for war! To blatantly destroy human life—especially an innocent—would send God's forces in the thousands, and they would fight, avenge the death by killing Aramus and the other elite. Belial would respond in kind, and Sardurvial understood that not only was he responsible for ruining the life of a precious woman, child and his loving mother, but also helped ignite the beginning stages of Armageddon. He damned the entire world!

"Sardurvial," a sad pleading voice said. "Please, I need you to wake, my friend."

The desperate tone of the calling voice roused Sardurvial's concern. Sardurvial sat up and gasped. His heavy eyes battled the surrounding haze. Someone large towered over him.

Sardurvial could only think of Belial. "Who?" he muttered, not feeling the present danger.

"Oh, thank God," the sad man towering over Sardurvial said, sniffing hard and wiping his eyes with the heels of his hands. "You frightened me, friend. You sleep like a log."

Sardurvial tried to focus but confusion distracted him. Didn't he just observe Aramus killing Kathy after he stepped from the boy's body?

"You must hurry and get up," the sad man said, his voice familiar to Sardurvial. He dug at his eyes in an attempt to clear the cloud, and then took a moment to examine the man standing over him. A sword sat in its sheath and rested on his hip, its great length trailing behind him. Sardurvial instantly knew who this man was. Only one was capable of brandishing such a rapier. It was his longtime friend, Jesseth, and somehow he was able to survive the onslaught of the townspeople and was able to locate Sardurvial!

Sardurvial's mind suddenly shifted to the memories of his dream. He drunkenly wobbled as he tried to push himself to his feet.

He was so tired.

"The woman Kathy and the boy Jaiden," Sardurvial said. "I must check on them!"

Jesseth sniffled, and his voice cracked as he spoke. "I've already done so in my search for you.

They're both fine. I saw them resting soundly inside the apartment."

Sardurvial didn't notice Jesseth's tears or the tremble in his voice. His mind was far away, inside the horrible memories of his dream. He shook his head in disagreement. The dream he had and its implication was more than just his mind running wild. They were not resting soundly as Jesseth had claimed. They were in terrible danger and needed to be protected. Maybe Jesseth's senses had been somehow fooled into believing such, but Sardurvial knew better. He needed to check on them and do so without delay.

"Sardurvial?" Jesseth said.

Sardurvial remained silent in his own deliberation.

"Trust in what I tell you," Jesseth said. "The woman and child are fine! Something terrible has happened to our brother Abraham. He has died, Sardurvial. His death was awful."

Sardurvial's expression failed. Immediately he felt the loss of his friend. Jesseth began to blubber. "Awful," he reiterated. "Me and Ishmael witnessed the entire thing. After we escaped those who chased us, we found each other deep in the forest, miles away from town. We didn't know where you and Abraham had gone or if either of you were even alive. We were desperate to figure things out, but everything felt so out of control. Our uncertainty and fear brought us to tears. What were we going to do? But then I heard something distant. It sounded like a thousand jumbled voices. I hushed Ishmael and we listened. I was right. I'd heard the shouts of a riotous crowd and the cries of one man's plea for help. Reluctant to see who it was that had gotten caught we decided to chance our own fate to investigate. Using the cover of the trees and stealth movement, we were able to draw dangerously close. It was terrible what we witnessed, Sardurvial!"

Jesseth dropped his head and fought through tears and emotion to share the rest of his experience.

"They were torturing Abraham! They were pulling the limbs from his body and peeling away his skin. By God he cried to the Heavens, but never once did he waver to their requests. He remained strong through the entire ordeal, defiantly standing up to all those who surrounded him, even to Belial and Aramus themselves!

"When death took him, Aramus turned to where I and Ishmael were hiding and he demanded the townspeople get us. We split up, agreeing to meet back in the forest tonight. I promised Ishmael I wouldn't return without you! While the townspeople hunted me, I kept hearing them carrying on about how Belial was ready to commence the final war. We need to stick together and plan Belial and Aramus's demise. Come with me right now, we don't have much time!"

Sardurvial heard Jesseth's words and the severity behind them, but something within kept him calm and contemplative. He figured a way to get one of them now while they were alone. One by one, when they were least expecting it, they could get them.

Correlating memories from his dream and his current troubled feelings, Sardurvial desperately dashed by Jesseth and ran up the stairs. Nighttime had fallen and the streets were eerily barren; the rushing wind brushed Sardurvial's skin and left a stinging sensation on the surface. It was a feeling he barely noticed. A chill followed, racing down his back. This he felt and shuddered at its bite. Respectively dismissing it as the cold, Sardurvial unconsciously pushed on, unknowing what he really felt was a forewarning of bad things to come. Onwards he raced, immediately taking to the side of the building he'd been on during his dream. Upwards he ascended, Jesseth following closely and remaining quiet in his confusion.

The two settled at a height even with Kathy's bedroom window, an altitude that made it easy for the angelic creatures to peer within the blackened room. Sardurvial remained quiet as he searched the room and noted how it was easier for him to see inside the room now then when he searched to see things in his dream. The contents of the room were all visible as was Kathy lying restfully atop the bed.

Jesseth observed Sardurvial, his eyes went wide with worry. "You're acting strangely," Jesseth said.

Sardurvial paid him no mind. He was onto something, and it required his full attention. He merely enclosed his face within his hands and pressed his forehead against the window in an attempt to get a better look inside.

"What is it, Sardurvial?" Jesseth asked. His voice was soft, showing concern. He was desperate to be included in Sardurvial's search. He peered into the room, looking for the nameless.

Sardurvial continued to investigate, his focus still sharp, heightened for the moment; Jesseth's confusion and questions remained the furthest things from his mind.

Moments passed and Sardurvial continued his quiet scrutiny of the room.

"Sardurvial!" Jesseth said nearly shouting. He turned quickly to face Sardurvial and his sword swung from his hip and tinged loudly as it bounced off the cement wall. Sardurvial threw an unfriendly glance at Jesseth.

"Quiet!"

Sardurvial resumed his search.

Where is the boy? Where is the body Aramus is hiding in?

"Sardurvial!" Jesseth shouted, his tolerance all but drained. "There are things more pressing than this that needs to be taken care of. And now!" He reached out and vigorously shook Sardurvial's shoulder, insistent on being acknowledged.

Sardurvial didn't turn to face Jesseth. He shrugged of his touch and spoke while he kept his focus within the house. "You woke me from a disturbing dream, Jesseth. One I cannot dismiss as being creations of a wild imagination. Aramus is within the little boy's body. He's hiding out, waiting for his assigned time to strike down the woman. You said it yourself; Belial is ready to wage war. Having the woman executed would gain Heaven's attention. Surely the Seraphs would be sent. You said we needed to plan Belial and Aramus's demise. We might be able to get one of them right now while he's outnumbered and vulnerable."

Jesseth was quiet and his focus switched to the conceivable: Aramus was within the boy's body. "Are you sure? Do you see the boy within the room?"

Sardurvial shook his head. "No, he's not there yet."

"Then let's go in," Jesseth said, and he unsheathed his sword. "We can wait for him in a darkened corner and surprise him when he comes for the woman, or we can get him when he sleeps. Whichever opportunity we're given."

"No," Sardurvial said. "Kathy is awake and the boy is too. He went to the kitchen. He's gone to get her something to eat and he's going to bring it back on a breakfast tray. Everything is playing out just like it did in my dream. I think it best if we wait here and let it run its course."

CHAPTER 21

TRUTH WITHIN LIES

Monday, October 17th, 1:44 am

Jaiden Michael shuffled down the hallway holding a breakfast tray. Carefully arranged silverware rattled with each progressing footstep and the glass of warm milk centered on the tray swirled dangerously close to spilling over the rim of the glass. Jaiden was proud of the meal he prepared for his aunt and he continued to concentrate on balancing the tray because bringing it to her flawless might help improve her mood.

It was good Jaiden was able to occupy himself because his host was unable to give him his undivided attention like he'd been able to do since he entered his body the night before. The host was extremely nervous about the coming events and was unsure what the outcome would be. The possibilities were limitless and nothing good would happen this night, he was certain of that. He was facing a powerful foe strong enough to kill with a thought, but this was the whole reason he befriended the boy and entered his body to begin with. He could only hope his reckless act would pay off and the element of surprise would work to his advantage.

Monday, October 17th, 1:44 am

Sardurvial and Jesseth continued to hover outside Kathy's bedroom window. The two were quietly observing Jaiden Michael as he casually strolled into the bedroom with a breakfast tray in hand. His bright boy's smile and childlike behavior could fool just about anyone. And for the moment, it had Sardurvial questioning his dreams authenticity. If Aramus was within the body, he was hiding himself well because he couldn't feel him and usually there was a noticeable sign that could be picked up right away. It could be a detectable awkwardness in the way the unfamiliar body was being carried or a speech impediment. Most hosting a body were usually unable to cover their own aroma. Every individual that fell from the Heavens has a unique smell that could easily be tracked, at least by other angels. Trained dogs can do it to people, and the heightened senses of an angel were far more developed than any canine.

Sardurvial continued to inspect the boy for any signs of Aramus being within his body. There wasn't a trace. For now, he figured he would remain outside the window and continue to wait for any indication that Aramus was there, hiding within the body. He was bound to slip up if he was confined within, and Sardurvial mulled a plan just in case the contents of his dream held true.

"I don't sense Aramus within the boy," said Jesseth, bringing pause to Sardurvial's thoughts.

"I don't either," Sardurvial said, unconvinced Aramus wasn't occupying the body. "He's a devious bastard like Belial, and I'm not willing to just dismiss his absence because I can't sense him. I've got to keep reminding myself how sly he is. This woman that saved my life may be in danger because of me. I can't leave here until I'm sure."

"Why don't we hide ourselves from their eyes and enter the room," Jesseth said. "This way we can get close to the boy. If Aramus is within, he won't be able to keep us both from smelling him. Our nearness will likely make him nervous and he'll begin to sweat."

Sardurvial went over Jesseth's plan. He liked it but was well aware of its flaws. Discouraged by the complications of it, he shook his head. "For some reason, I think the woman can sense me when I'm near, even when I don't want her to. I think Belial did something to my influence when he went to her while she slept last night and showed her events from the past. I know he planned these events long before the woman was even born. I should've foreseen it, but I was blind to his games and distorted views when I served him like a mindless dog. I'll cherish the day he's destroyed!"

Jesseth smiled, pleased. "I look forward to that day myself. But for now, if we both work to shield the woman from being able to see us then I really believe she won't be able to regardless of what Belial has done to her senses."

Sardurvial contemplated Jesseth's confidence in their abilities to fend off Belial's influence. Sardurvial truly felt Jesseth was underestimating Belial's power and looked to say so but thought better of it. What choice did they have really? They couldn't leave until they knew for sure Aramus wasn't around, and moving in close seemed to be the only way to force his hand. They lost their friend Abraham, and Ishmael was waiting for their return inside Hells' forest alone.

"Okay then," Sardurvial said, deciding it must be as Jesseth said. "But let us be swift in our scrutiny and be sure to shield the woman of our presence.

I've caused this woman enough anguish and the last thing I want to do is cause her any more pain. She needs to begin the healing process."

Together, Sardurvial and Jesseth entered the bedroom through the wall. With the two working constantly to block Kathy's awareness of their nearness, she lay ignorant to their coming. Knowing their attempts to shield Kathy's perception was working, the two walked around the side of the bed and kept their attention on the boy, examining him closely.

If Aramus was still within the body, Sardurvial couldn't sense it and was going to have to move closer to put pressure on him.

Jaiden shifted uncomfortably, sidestepping to the tray he'd moved to the night table when Kathy finished her meal. Grabbing a knife from the tray and hiding it against his side, Jaiden looked nervously out of the corner of his eye. Sardurvial didn't notice the boy take a weapon, but Jesseth did and he stepped forward, sending the boy scurring back a few steps. Sardurvial paused in indecision.

"Are you okay Jaiden?" Kathy said.

Jaiden's expression tightened and beads of sweat formed on his brow.

"Thank you for the food, it was great," Kathy said. "But it's getting late. Why don't you try and lie down now and get some sleep? I think a good night's rest will do us wonders."

Jaiden nodded his head in accordance but didn't move. Jesseth stepped forward and Sardurvial sensed something he didn't like. Sardurvial watched and studied, unable to see what Jesseth was up to.

"What is it?" Sardurvial whispered and continued to search the boy. He couldn't seem to locate what Jesseth was locked on.

Jesseth paused and slowly raised his sword, pointing it at the boy. He whispered to Sardurvial without taking his eyes off the boy. "I thought I sensed Aramus hiding within the boy's body, but I don't think he's there. Maybe it's just that I was hoping he was there because I want to kill him because he betrayed us."

Tense moments passed before Jesseth lowered his sword and turned his back to the boy. "But he's not here, I'm absolutely certain of it, Sardurvial."

Relieved to find Kathy and Jaiden were safe, Sardurvial felt the tension leave. Now he and the others could concentrate on confronting Belial before he did something foolish. Then they would deal with Aramus, the lesser of the two evils.

"Good," Sardurvial said. "Let's get a move on and meet with Ishmael. Let's plan Belial's demise."

Jesseth smiled, approving of Sardurvial's plan and Sardurvial smiled back in confidence. The two seemed to be harmonizing.

"I would like to assist you in that task, really, but I can't allow that to happen," Jesseth said.

Sardurvial's smile faded. "What?"

"It's your demise that has been planned today." Jesseth spun around and swung his sword in one uninterrupted motion towards Jaiden. The movement was blurry to Sardurvial's superior eyesight and far quicker than his thought process.

Aramus quickly leapt from the boy's body, protecting its soft shell from the razor sharp blade Jesseth swung. The blade didn't hesitate as it sliced Aramus's belly open and began spilling his blood out onto the floor. Aramus gasped and cradled his abdomen, holding the gaping wound together with a panicked grasp.

With Aramus outside the boy's body now, Jaiden came to and dropped the knife and ran for his aunt's arms. She accepted him with open arms and rocked him back and forth. "Let it all out baby it's okay. I miss her too!"

Sardurvial was surprised that Aramus was inside the boy and that Jesseth knew. In the unfolding moments, he found concern for the boy and his current condition, but also found relief seeing Aramus on the floor incapacitated. They would kill him because of what he stood for. This was war and war had casualties. He quickly moved between Jesseth and Aramus and looked down on him. The combination of pity and anger kept Sardurvial from striking his old friend.

"Let the deep wound bleed," Sardurvial said. "I hope you can feel the suffering like the people do."

Aramus gasped and choked. "I can't keep my hold over Kathy's emotions," Aramus said.

"Good," Sardurvial said. "Let them see you for what you are."

Kathy's eyes moved to Sardurvial standing over Aramus. She screamed and struggled to roll off the soft bed, Jaiden held tight in her arms.

Sardurvial turned and faced Kathy, realizing he let go of the hold he had over her emotions. He looked at Jesseth and saw his attention was still firmly on Aramus. It was apparent he let go of his hold over Kathy's emotions too. He returned his attention back to Kathy. He could see and feel her fear and he was unable to gain control of it. She was shaking and he stepped to comfort her, to tell her how she needed to calm down, that they were going to keep her and her nephew safe from ever being in harm's way again.

"It's okay Kathy," Sardurvial said. "We're going to protect you. Jesseth and I—" he turned and pointed at Jesseth and was stopped by something that made him think. "We're going to . . ."

He looked down, his belly burning.

A long silver object was lodged in his belly and extended outwards. His eyes followed the object outwards and he stopped at a pair of rough looking hands that wrapped the swords stately handle. He knew exactly whose hands those are.

"Jesseth?"

Sardurvial blinked heavily, his thoughts jumbled by pain. He raised his eyes to meet Jesseth's. His friend's eyes contained such inexplicable anger.

But why?

Sardurvial opened his mouth to ask that question but spit blood instead.

He hurt.

Terribly.

He stepped back, dislodging himself from the blade. Hot blood pumped out of his wound and soaked his shirt. Knee buckling pain rolled his eyes into the back of his head and he dropped to the floor. Pain and confusion continued to consume him.

Kathy turned her back to the chaos and cradled Jaiden tightly in her arms, shielding his eyes from the violence around them.

"You're a fool, Sardurvial," Jesseth said. Wiping the blood from the blade with his fingers, he ran his stained fingers down his cheeks. "And Aramus is a fool too for thinking he could scheme behind my back."

Jesseth turned the sword on himself, sinking the tip of the blade into the skin above the bellybutton. Showing no pain, he slowly dragged the blade upwards. Losing no blood, the sword stopped just underneath the chin. Dropping the sword, Jesseth placed his hands inside the incision and peeled away the skin. Stepping out of the flesh as if it were a tailored suit, it dropped to the floor and flopped like it were made from rubber.

Belial reached down and picked up the sword; twirling it masterfully, he inspected it with high consideration. "You know, Jesseth brandished a highly powerful weapon! I didn't realize what a work of art it was. It is one of the first weapons I forged with my own hands and I thought at the time it was an inferior piece. What little I knew then."

Sardurvial swallowed hard in an attempt to embrace the pain that burned his belly. His wound looked bad but by no means did it completely incapacitate him. *Be patient,* he thought. *Belial will need to share his story. His pretentiousness could never go undisclosed. What would his careful planning mean unless it was fully understood by everyone it was designed to hurt? It would mean nothing, and Belial wouldn't allow such a scheme to go fully unnoticed and unappreciated.*

Sardurvial remained still, playing possum until the perfect moment to act presented itself.

Belial smiled snidely. "You gather in the forest, hiding like scared children, sharing stories and making plans against me. Were you all foolish enough to think I wouldn't find out? Fools! All the times you gathered there, I was around, listening and scheming against you all the while you thought you were scheming against me. Aramus pretended to be angered by your story inside the forest; somehow he sensed my nearness and he quickly turned. It was his sad attempt to cover his true feelings and to try and convince me he never broke my law. But I know better to trust anyone other than myself, always have. So I guess you're wondering what I'm going to do next."

Belial laughed heartily. He looked at Kathy and then at the boy. Disdain and humor kept his expression neutral.

Sardurvial followed Belial's eyes curiously as they roamed to Aramus and then back to himself. "I'll answer that question but only to satisfy my need to hurt you worse than you've attempted to hurt me and my empire. I am going to kill the woman and child as I did Jesseth because I am ready for war. But don't fuss. Some of you never had the chance to share in this glorious moment. I planned these events long ago. Every single breath of it. From Kathy and Rocco to Megan and Ted. Lenny and Redhead to Tyler. And all of that planning has brought us to this moment."

Aramus groaned in his pain.

"Keep quiet while I'm talking," Belial said. "Removing Jesseth's guts so I could fit inside his flesh was a bit gross. He was alive during most of the process and he screamed out with such displeasure. He was as weak in death as he was in life. Please, Sardurvial, don't be the same as him. Have some dignity."

Belial raised the sword over his head, shrugged his shoulders indifferently and cringed as he pulled the blade down with all of his might towards Sardurvial's neck. Sardurvial closed his eyes and looked away, accepting his fate. In the passing moment between the sword leaving Belial's shoulder and it moving quickly to slash through his skull, Sardurvial willingly submitted his life in exchange for complete forgiveness of his past deeds. What he saw before him was a callous cold-hearted beast that he tried to model himself after, and because of that, he felt eternally tainted and shamed.

"Please forgive me."

A meat smacking thump and a blur before Sardurvial left him still for a moment. He found himself waiting for something significant, like death to come. But for the moment he felt unchanged.

He stared cognitively at the horizontal splatter of blood on the floor before him. He couldn't help but think how that was a strange projection for his blood to spurt.

A crash off to his side turned his head, and that was when he realized that was not his blood on the ground. Belial and Aramus were tussling, wrestling for the sword. Aramus was bleeding terribly, his insides were hanging out of the gaping wound but his fight was unremitting.

"Take the woman and get her to safety," Aramus said, his struggle with Belial made the appeal sound desperate.

Then, in a wave of flashbacks, Sardurvial understood what Aramus was doing. In the forest that day when everything began to fall apart, Sardurvial punched Aramus and split his lip, Aramus didn't fight back. And during that first attack Aramus led after their dissent, Aramus was the one who ordered the townspeople to back away from Sardurvial. He claimed he wanted Sardurvial for himself. This presented Sardurvial the perfect opportunity to escape. And in the kitchen, Aramus quickly disappeared when Kathy drew near.

Aramus was biding his friend's time to escape while he placed himself in imminent danger entertaining Belial.

Sardurvial turned to Kathy. "Please, Kathy, you two must come with me!" He looked at her with compassion and stretched his hand out to her.

Hesitant at first, she took his hand, and while protecting Jaiden within the serenity of a tight hug, she said, "Please, Sam, help us through this, we're terrified."

Sardurvial paused in a timeless moment. Hard choices were made. With the success of this newly formed plan, he was guaranteed fulfillment. Sardurvial said nothing in response to the woman's plea. He merely cherished the open femininity of it and the pure innocence it radiated. She was precious and he would reward her for the trust she'd given him again. But this time it meant so much more because he didn't influence it.

Finally, there was closure.

"Belial!" Sardurvial shouted, and he turned away from Kathy and Jaiden to face him. Belial paused his fight, and Aramus dropped to the floor beaten and barely alive. Belial stood upright with not a bead of sweat faulting his forehead. He wiped the blood from his knuckles and retrieved the sword from the floor by his feet. This was the moment he'd been waiting for. This was the true moment behind his careful planning. He stared inquisitively at Sardurvial and raised an expectant eyebrow.

"I was wrong, Belial," Sardurvial's voice quivered. "I was wrong for ever having gone against your word. I was wrong for ever having questioned your leadership over these people. They are weak and I want to earn my way back into your good graces. Kill Aramus and kill the woman and boy in exchange for my impious ways. Please have mercy on me! I will fight for you, make all the wrong I've done right!"

Kathy's mouth hung open and she lowered Jaiden to the floor. "How could you!" she erupted, her tone convicting, this betrayal as bad as the one that took her husband's life. She began to blubber. Her life had been a series of tragedies, so why should today be any different?

Belial smiled in delight; his plan to make all those around Sardurvial suffer until he returned home worked. He no longer had concern over the fate of the other's that escaped; they were free to do as they wished. Now, while favor was on his side and he could prove to his followers that God was imperfect, he needed to act.

"Tell me you mean what you say, Sardurvial," Belial demanded.

"I mean what I say Belial. I beg you for a second chance."

"There will be conditions," Belial said and he stepped forward, the sword held out before him, the tip aimed at Kathy throat. Slow and precise Belial marched towards Kathy. Kathy remained as still as she could, but she continued to cry in the face of death. Her throat rocked dangerously close to the tip of the blade. "I hate these damn people." Belial paused to savor the moment and let Kathy's fear feed his blackened soul. He lowered the sword to the center of her chest, and then he looked to where Sardurvial was standing and, there, he found Kathy. Confusion filled Belial. He looked to the person standing at the end of his sword and it was Sardurvial.

"I've fooled you, Belial. You're imperfect. You've allowed your student to get one over on you, to trick you with simple deceit. But I suppose I was taught by the master of deceit, wasn't I?"

Sardurvial pushed Jaiden to Kathy and leapt forward, impaling himself on the sword held outright. Belial's eyes went wide as he felt the pain of the death-blow and looked into Sardurvial's wide distancing gaze. Surprisingly enough, the smile on Sardurvial's face never faded. He endured the pain he was feeling in appreciation for the pleasure this moment brought him. He was content dying here, unknowing exactly what dying meant to him. He outwitted Belial and he sacrificed himself for a greater love. It was for the love of his God he left behind so long ago, and for the love of a woman and child he'd caused so much pain. He knew with his pain and passing she was not cured, but she was out of this now. Given a chance to continue to live and love again. And she would, he believed, because the Heavens acknowledged her.

Belial howled out in anguish and tried to withdraw the sword in an attempt to turn it on the woman. Sardurvial grabbed the handle and sunk the sword in deeper, turning it to speed death's approach.

"You've failed here on more than one account, Belial. Live with it." Sardurvial spat, and blood began pouring from his mouth. His grip began to loosen until there was no strength left within him. Slumping forward in death, Belial was finally able to withdraw the sword. Sardurvial fell to the floor limply, a satisfied smile remaining.

Belial dropped the sword. Turning to see Kathy and Jaiden comforted within the arms of a woman he'd long since forgotten about. He snickered. He still hated the sight of Porcelain Face.

"Sardurvial has ascended to the Heavens already. Aramus has departed to seek those that have escaped the forest, and you are finished here. Haven't you learned that you cannot begin the final war on your terms? God wants His people closer and you continue to help him with that cause. He's not quite ready to end your suffering yet. Little by little your empire will shrink and when you realize all is lost, you'll try to come back to Him. You'll suffer eternally if you don't forfeit this imprudent plan to make better what He has already made perfect. What you will do tomorrow has already been foreseen."

"And what I will do," Belial said, his hate tangible, "is prove that I am supreme. I still have the Definitive Amassment. I only need to make God wrong on one account out of trillions. How hard could that be? I will eventually be able to find that one person in that book that I can mold to my will and control their destiny. I can prove God isn't flawless. Let the others run for now and let this woman and child live their lowly miserable lives. I care nothing about that. There are still two others from the forest that I still have to work with. I'll start with them. They'll help me rise to glory!"

Belial stepped into the shadows and he melded with them, disappearing from the eyes of the physical world. Disappointed phase one of his plan didn't work, he returned home to start on the design of his next plan that would exalt his throne most high. He would tell his townspeople he hunted the dissenters and killed them as an example. In time he would figure a way to get Aramus and Ishmael, and when he did, they would know suffering and would gladly return to his side! And when that happened, his point that God wasn't perfect would have been made. What better way to dethrone Him? He could win so many over to his side with such incriminating evidence.

CHAPTER 22

LOVE

Monday, October 17th, 9:01 am

Kathy sat in bed with her back against the headboard. Her attention was within herself, searching for the thing that woke her suddenly. It wasn't a threatening thump or a foreign sound, rather it was peaceful, like a tugging on her heart. It was trying to tell her something but what exactly that was, she couldn't quite finger. Strangely, it wasn't pain or sorrow because the sadness had completely left her.

Her search continued but went unresolved.

She leaned forward and looked to her side and saw Jaiden lying next to her, sleeping soundly. The bed blankets wrapped his body, covering him almost completely. She smiled down on him and pushed away the covers that blocked his face. She couldn't help but notice how innocent and vulnerable he looked.

Why couldn't the world be simple like a sleeping child?

Because everything was broken.

Kathy understood she was now solely responsible for Jaiden. Though the details were cloudy and unimportant, most of what happened to her sister and Jaiden's father was fresh in her mind. She was sure it was going to be in her nephew's mind once he woke as well. Not enough days of mourning had gone by to enervate the pain that would undoubtedly fill his young heart. It was going to take time and a lot of love and nurturing for him to come to terms. But he would be fine, she was absolutely certain of that.

Knowing things would work themselves out, Kathy smiled contentedly and allowed herself to sink into the bed. Suddenly realizing the pain in her back completely disappeared like her grief, she turned to her right and discovered a vibrant bouquet of healthy flowers on her night table. Its sudden and mysterious presence didn't cause her any concern. Rather, it filled her with an unexplainable sense of security and love.

Love.

She couldn't help but think the flowers being there meant blue skies would be welcoming both her and Jaiden to each new day. She saw a white piece of paper held in the colored cluster of plant life. She removed it and inspected the envelope for a greeting. Not finding one, she opened it and removed the card within. Kathy was absorbed by the drawing on the card of a male and female angel holding hands, hovering above the earth and smiling down on the quiet city below.

It was as if they were smiling down on her.

She opened the card to find a beautifully scribed message:

Sharing the love that has filled your heart and allowing it to guide you will get you through whatever obstacle you might face in life. This is what it has done for one believed lost forever . . .

-Angela

A tingling sensation that was pleasure-filled and perfect coursed through Kathy's body. Without questioning the reasons why, she placed the card back where she found it, and sunk beneath the covers and closed her eyes. Maybe, she thought as she began to drift into sleep again, she would be able to dream of nothing but pleasant things like Megan and Rocco being in a better place.

PART II

EPILOGUE

CHAPTER 23

HEAVEN

Lying prone, Sardurvial began to stir. He struggled to open his heavy eyelids only to find he was encased in an impenetrable darkness. Where he was and how long he'd been in this strange location was a mystery. The last thing he remembered was pulling the sword Belial intended to use on Kathy into his own belly and the sparks of pain that followed.

He sacrificed himself for love.

To make a departing statement to Belial, he remembered grabbing the handle of the sword and twisting it. That's when the pain became satisfyingly numbing. And now that he reflected on the moment, he was glad to know he was able to prove to himself that he really had changed into something better than what he'd been before. He now understood and respected the value of human life and the power of love.

Sardurvial recognized a void within. This void was, until his sacrifice, filled with hatred and animosity, but now it was empty, the love that had taken its place somehow gone. The need to refill it was like a belly filled with hunger pains. Only the hunger pains he was experiencing were feelings of loneliness and vulnerability of becoming what he once was again. It frightened him to think the love had left him forever because he was undeserving of its powerful embrace.

He wondered where it could have gone and if it could ever be reclaimed.

As if love heard his thoughts, it made its presence known through a warm swooping breeze that passed through him and moved onwards. Though it didn't go far, it was lying in wait somewhere beyond the walls that confined him, waiting to be reclaimed. He wanted to go and get it, take hold of it and never let it go. To do so he knew he must stand, but was unsure if he actually could. The wound he had suffered was bad. He brought his legs towards his chest and paused to assess the feeling.

He sighed in relief.

He felt no pain.

Sardurvial reached down and brushed his hand over his belly to try and locate the wound the sword created. The mortal wound had miraculously healed and left no trace of having been there.

His physical condition—like his current location—mystified him, but his need to find the lost love motivated him. He slowly pushed himself to his feet, moving carefully, as if he were to do anything too quickly the love that was lying in wait would hear his approach and scamper away. He shivered at the thought and began to walk aimlessly, his eyes wide in desperate search for an ounce of light that might reveal his whereabouts or the way out.

Worry strangled his lungs and sweat beaded his forehead. Sardurvial panted in desperation. There seemed to be nothing around him. He couldn't help but think this might be his everlasting punishment, to spend eternity alone in complete darkness and silence, lost forever without forgiveness and just out of love's reach with it calling for him, begging him onwards. He whimpered.

The love called to him: *Don't give up.*

A troubled sob escaped his lips.

He desired love.

"I am sorry!" he wailed. "I can do no more to right the wrongs if this is where I am condemned to spend eternity!"

His voice echoed and faded. The silence he got in return was hope shattering.

His soul trembled.

Just then something in the surrounding darkness banged. Sardurvial searched with desperation, straining his eyes to find what it was. "Who's there?" he asked, his voice distrustful.

"Sardurvial, is that you?" someone called. It was distant and echoed, sounding like it came from forever and forever seemed so far away.

Unsure of its location, Sardurvial spun and searched the murky air with widened eyes. Unable to decipher anything in the bleak blackness, he decided even if it was Belial calling him, he would respond and face whatever might come from it. Inevitability left him that undesired choice. Because he knew in order to escape the darkness, he must have someone show him the way out. He cupped his hands around his mouth, and shouted into forever, "It is me! I don't know where I am and it is so dark I can't see an inch in front of my face."

Rattling filled Sardurvial's ears.

Though still unable to see anything, he was finally able to discern the direction the sound was coming from and he stared in that direction defensively. Taking a step away for the sake of security, he waited.

A door swung open and light flooded the massive white room he was standing in. He squinted and struggled against the impossible brightness of the light behind the body and hid it in shadow.

"I've been waiting for you to wake, Sardurvial," the approaching man shouted, but his voice remained silent until he neared. "It is all so beautiful. Wait until you see how things have changed."

Sardurvial was speechless as he stared confusedly into Jesseth's eyes. He died by Belial's hands and yet he stood there before him?

"Are we in Heaven?"

An exultant smile spread across Jesseth's face. He patted his shoulder. "Come with me, Sardurvial. We've been waiting long for you to wake and now that you have, we should go without delay. I'm sure Ishmael and Aramus are scared, alone and in hiding. I'm sure they can use our help."

"Aramus . . ." Sardurvial muttered pensively.

Abraham entered the room. He smiled sprightly at Sardurvial and he unfettered a deep chuckle from the pit of his belly as he wrapped his arms tightly around Sardurvial. He picked him up and twirled him around and around.

"Aye," Abraham groaned in satisfaction. "I've missed you, chap! I can't tell you how good it makes me feel to see you again!"

Sardurvial was placed down and he mindlessly clapped Abraham's back. His emotions were mixed and they kept him distant. Confusion as to how this all unfolded clashed with the delight of having been reunited with his friends. He was unable to put together any of the events succeeding the pain of being impaled on Belial's sword. Withdrawn, he turned away from Abraham and continued his silent contemplation.

Jesseth and Abraham shared an open smile. "Should we tell him?" Jesseth asked Abraham, and Sardurvial watched the two deliberate with uncertainty.

Abraham approached Sardurvial and placed an arm around his shoulder. He led him towards the light. "Aye, I say it better if we just show him."

Abraham led Sardurvial through the door and into the source of the brilliant light.

Sardurvial found it bright, but not so that it bothered his eyes like it did when Jesseth first came for him. It was soft and warm, welcoming and comfortable. He closed his eyes and tilted his head back, allowing the invisible energy to seep into his pores. He'd found the love, and it was filling his heart, chasing away his fear and sorrow.

"I want to stay here and feel like this forever," Sardurvial whispered trancelike.

Jesseth smiled in appreciation, and Abraham gently pulled Sardurvial along. "We know you do," Abraham said. "You've forgotten how consuming God's love is, haven't you?"

Sardurvial stopped and studied his friend's faces. He found they were both smiling brightly—as bright as the light they'd been standing in. "God?" Sardurvial said; his voice filled with hope.

Abraham nodded and added the exclamation point. "God!"

Sardurvial's heart pounded and his mouth instantly dried. "How is that so?"

"It is amazing, isn't it?" Jesseth said. "We're all here again in spite of what we've done. We're being given a second chance."

"But the law says we can never return!"

"And yet here we are. Only by the grace of God could this happen."

Sardurvial tried to absorb Jesseth's words as he listened to him continuing to talk about the miraculous way they were reunited. He began to follow Abraham and was frustrated by the slow pace he maintained. He quickened his steps in an attempt to hurry them, knowing when he reached his final destination he would finally understand the reasons why. Though he had an idea as to where he was, to truly believe he was actually there was something else entirely.

Abraham and Jesseth stopped before a cloaked door. "We're here! You won't believe what you're about to see, Sardurvial. But we're here! Are you ready for this?"

Sardurvial swallowed hard in nervous anticipation, and then nodded in approval. He knew contemplation would only delay things further.

Jesseth pulled the door open, and in that instant, Sardurvial felt as though he was ascending, and doing so rapidly. His head felt as if it was spinning and his belly was somewhere in his feet. He sucked a deep breath so he could scream for his life, but the sudden jolt of being brought to an abrupt halt took away what wind he gathered.

"The fall," he said, finding himself on his hands and knees. "It felt exactly like that, but instead of going down, I felt like I was going up."

Sardurvial pushed himself to his feet; his movement was sluggish and testing. Unsure if he was just stunned or if he was hurt in any way, he kept his focus on the ground around his feet because it helped to steady his head and calm his stomach.

Rustling sounds beyond him, which were purposely being kept quiet, escaped his attention as he tried to assess his body's condition.

Realizing he was just shaken a bit, Sardurvial lifted his chin in an attempt to locate the sounds' whereabouts and was stunned by what he saw.

Angels, a countless amount, were seated before Sardurvial and were watching him. Their expressions were blank and shrouded by a darkness that was outside the lighted stage he found himself on. Behind the mass of bodies were windows, large and dynamically curved. Their shape gave Sardurvial the impression the room he was in was a sphere and it was immense. Outside the room, beyond the glass windows, the lights of a distant city could be seen. Sardurvial didn't recognize the scenery or any of the shrouded faces staring back at him. He turned to explore the rest of the room, and to his surprise, he found someone on the stage with him.

Instantly consumed with humbling fear and a hundred other spirit-breaking emotions, Sardurvial dropped to his knees and quivered while he begged for mercy and forgiveness. The One seated on a throne before him remained unresponsive by voice. He merely waved His hand in the air, motioning for action.

Abraham and Jesseth rushed from the shadows and helped Sardurvial to stand. Weakened and afraid by what he saw, Sardurvial's legs couldn't find the strength he needed to hold his body upright.

"Aye, Sardurvial," Abraham muttered. "Gather yourself, chap, and face the Lord with the respect He deserves."

Sardurvial adhered to Abraham's request and quieted his internal cries and gathered his strength.

"I'm okay," he said, and they backed away, leaving him alone, standing face to face with God. His knees trembled and his hands quivered with little control, but nevertheless, he managed to remain standing. Shy in his evaluation, Sardurvial looked into God's soft eyes and saw the love and compassion he so willingly walked away from and so desperately sought when he was trapped in that darkened room.

Knowing words couldn't make up for the time lost and the pain he had caused, Sardurvial bowed his head in shame and remained uncomfortably silent. A thousand lifetimes of bad decisions brought him to this moment, and he could only hope God's judgment was swift.

"Welcome home, Sardurvial," God said.

Sardurvial slowly raised his head in question.

God smiled. "I always knew you'd come back to me."

The angels seated around began to applaud, and one by one, they stood in their ovation to welcome Sardurvial home. He spun and watched those he never had a chance to know and love with the same confusion and shame he felt when God made His presence known.

Why would they welcome him when he'd done nothing but betray their God, defy their way of life and harm His people?

This question overcame Sardurvial and compelled him to return his attention to God.

God raised a hand and brought silence to the applause. Lowering His hand, in unison, the angels sat.

"This moment is a celebration of your return to me, Sardurvial," God said. His voice was sympathetic and His expression kind. "But to fully appreciate the moment, I suppose you must understand the reasons why. Please, have a seat before me."

A seat appeared beside Sardurvial and he sat.

"The very first day my angels began to wish for freewill, I mourned a great loss. I knew granting the foolish desires of my children would only turn them away from me, allow them to feel jealousy and self-righteousness and, eventually, destructive unsound hatred. But I knew I couldn't deny anyone their feelings or change what was to be. I set that rule, and because of that, there was a need on a personal level for my angels to learn and grow on their own, to make decisions separate from my guidance, to know that I truly loved them without limits as I do my people. And to also understand that sometimes when you think something someone possesses is a gift, and then come to possess it yourself, you realize the hardships and understand what they have is really no gift at all.

"It is a burden, this gift, and at times, a curse. Love can overpower the deepest unsound hatred. It's that powerful. I created it to be that way. And now that you have seen that, Sardurvial, just like Abraham, Jesseth, Ishmael and Aramus have, you have all come back to me like I always knew you would. You've realized this is your proper place. But I want to make one thing very clear. Though I know the outcome of everything, what you were granted before you fell and what you still make decisions with is that burden I call freewill. It is a delicate gift; handle it with extreme care because the decisions you make, good or bad, and the consequences that they will bring are and will be forevermore your burden. Now stand before me, Sardurvial."

Sardurvial stood and the seat vanished.

"So now you are home and I ask only one thing of you."

"Anything Lord," Sardurvial said.

"Don't ever take love for granted again. It's far too precious."

Sardurvial nodded. "It is."

"That's the way it was meant to be."

"What will become of Aramus?"

"He will be home soon."

Sardurvial went to speak but stopped himself.

"What is it?" God said.

"What about the girl? What about Redhead?"

God smiled. "I'm glad you asked. She was merely just a pawn to open your eyes and bring you back home. Angelina, come forward."

Angelina stepped on the stage and bowed at God. She looked at Sardurvial. "I would pretend to be a little girl and die a thousand deaths if it meant helping the people and my kin."

Belial entered the steam room and Lenny was sitting on the stone bench.

"We have much work to do," Belial said.

"I am ready," Lenny said.

"There's some people I'd like you to influence."

Lenny stood. "Tell me what you need me to do."

"Bring out their evil, break them emotionally, make them kill and bring them to me when you're done with them."

Lenny turned with a smile. "I can do that."

"The worse they are, the more we can use them."

"I have so many ideas," Lenny said, and exited the steam room with his laughter echoing loudly.

Belial grabbed the Definitive Amassment and flipped through its aging pages. "I see now that this was just a distraction."

He lit the book on fire and watched it burn until it was reduced to ash.

"I'll get a thousand like Lenny and a hundred thousand more and nothing will distract me from the path of destruction I must make to prove him fallible. Nothing!!"

BOOKS BY
KEITH ROMMEL

Thanatology Series

The Cursed Man

The Lurking Man

The Sinful Man

The Silent Woman

Among the People

Devil Tree Series

The Devil Tree

The Devil Tree II

The White River Monster

Ice Canyon Monster